The Turn of The Crystal

The cavern was in confusion as they retreated
back into the inner cave. The sound of the
swords echoed, counterpointed by Meliadus's
enraged shouts.
Hawkmoon dragged the wounded Mygan back
to the second cave, warding off the blows that
fell upon them both.
Now Hawkmoon faced the singing blade of
Meliadus himself, who swung his sword
two-handed.
Hawkmoon felt a numbing shock in his left
shoulder, felt blood begin to soak his sleeve.
He parried a further blow, taking Meliadus in
the arm. The baron groaned and staggered back.
'Now, D'Averc!' called Hawkmoon. 'Now,
Mygan! Turn the crystals! It is our only hope
of escape!'
He turned the crystal in his ring first to the
right and then to the left, then six times more to
right and left.
And then Meliadus had vanished.
So had the cavern, so had his friends.
He stood alone on a plain that stretched flat in
all directions . . .

Also available in Mayflower Books,
in the Champion Eternal series:

*Interconnected series

The Sword of the Dawn

The History of the Runestaff:
Volume Three

Michael Moorcock

Mayflower

Granada Publishing Limited
First published in 1969 by Mayflower Books Ltd
Frogmore, St Albans, Herts AL2 2NF
Reprinted 1969, 1972, 1973, 1974, 1975, 1977

Copyright © Michael Moorcock 1968
Made and printed in Great Britain by
Hunt Barnard Printing Ltd
Aylesbury, Bucks
Set in Monotype Times

For Ed and Leigh Brackett Hamilton

Contents

BOOK ONE

WHEN DORIAN HAWKMOON, last Duke of Köln, ripped the Red Amulet from the throat of the Mad God and made that powerful thing his own, he returned with Huillam D'Averc and Oladahn of the Mountains to the Kamarg where Count Brass, his daughter Yisselda, his friend Bowgentle the philosopher and all their people underwent siege from the hordes of the Dark Empire led by Hawkmoon's old enemy Baron Meliadus of Kroiden.

So powerful had the Dark Empire grown that it threatened to destroy even the well-protected province of the Kamarg. If that happened, it would mean that Meliadus would take Yisselda for his own and slay slowly all the rest, turning the Kamarg to a waste of ash. Only by the mighty force released by the ancient machine of the wraith-folk which could warp whole areas of time and space were they saved by shifting into another dimension of the Earth.

And so they found sanctuary. Sanctuary in some other Kamarg, where the evil and horror of Granbretan did not exist; but they knew that if ever the crystal machine were destroyed, they would be plunged back into the chaos of their own time and space.

For a while they lived in joyful relief at their escape. but gradually Hawkmoon began to finger his sword and wonder at the fate of his own world . . .

—The High History of the Runestaff

7

Chapter One
THE LAST CITY

THE GRIM RIDERS spurred their battle-steeds up the muddy slopes of the hill, coughing as their lungs took in the thick black smoke that rose from the valley.

It was evening, the sun was setting and their grotesque shadows were long. In the twilight, it seemed that gigantic beast-headed creatures rode the horses.

Each rider bore a banner, stained by war, each wore a huge beast-mask of jeweled metal and heavy armor of steel, brass and silver, emblazoned with its wearer's device, battered and bloodied, and each gauntleted right hand gripped a weapon on which was encrusted the remains of a hundred innocents.

The six horsemen reached the top of the hill and dragged their snorting mounts to a halt, stabbing their banners into the earth where they flapped like the wings of birds of prey in the hot wind from the valley.

Wolf-mask turned to stare at Fly-mask, Ape glanced at Goat, Rat seemed to grin at Hound – a grin of triumph. The Beasts of the Dark Empire, each a Warlord of thousands, looked beyond the valley and beyond the hills to the sea, looked back at the blazing city below them where, faintly, they could hear the wails of the slaughtered and the tormented.

The sun set, night fell and the flames burned brighter, reflected in the dark metal of the masks of the Lords of Granbretan.

"Well, my lords," said Baron Meliadus, Gran Constable of the Order of the Wolf, Commander of the Army of Conquest, his deep, vibrant voice booming from within his great mask, "well, we have conquered all Europe now."

Mygel Holst, skeletal Archduke of Londra, head of the Order of the Goat, laughed. "Aye – all Europe. Not an inch of it is not ours. And now great parts of the East belong to us also."

The Goat helm nodded as if in satisfaction, the ruby eyes catching the firelight, flashing malignantly.

"Soon," merrily growled Adaz Promp, Master of the Order of the Hound, "all the world will be ours. All."

The Barons of Granbretan, masters of a continent, tacticians and warriors of ferocious courage and skill, careless of their own lives, corrupt of soul and mad of brain, haters of all that was not in decay, wielders of power without morality, force without justice, chuckled with gloomy pleasure as they watched the last European city to withstand them crumble and die. It had been an old city. It had been called Athena.

"All," said Jerek Nankenseen, Warlord of the Order of the Fly, "save the hidden Kamarg . . ."

And Baron Meliadus lost his humor then, made almost as if he would strike his fellow warlord.

Jerek Nankenseen's bejeweled Fly-mask turned a little to regard Meliadus and the voice from within the mask was baiting. "Is it not enough that you have chased them away, my lord Baron?"

"No," snarled the Wolf of Wolves. "Not enough."

"They can offer us no menace," murmured Baron Brenal Farnu of the Rat helm. "From what our scientists divined, they exist in a dimension beyond Earth, in some other time or space. We cannot reach them and they cannot reach us. Let us enjoy our triumph, unmarred by thoughts of Hawkmoon and Count Brass . . ."

"I cannot!"

"Or is it another name that haunts thee, brother Baron?" Jerek Nankenseen mocked the man who had been his rival in more than one amorous encounter in Londra. "The name of the fair one, Yisselda? Is it *love* that moves you, my lord? Sweet love?"

For a moment the Wolf did not reply, but the hand that gripped the sword tightened as if in fury. Then the rich, musical voice spoke and it had recovered its composure, was almost light in tone.

"Vengeance, Baron Jerek Nankenseen, is what motivates me . . ."

"You are a most passionate man, Baron . . ." Jerek Nankenseen said dryly.

Meliadus sheathed his sword suddenly and reached out to

10

grasp his banner, wrenching it from the earth. "They have insulted our King-Emperor, our land – and myself. I will have the girl for my pleasure, but in no soft spirit will I take her, no weak emotion will motivate me . . ."

"Of course not," murmured Jerek Nankenseen, a hint of patronage in his voice.

". . . And as for the others, I will have my pleasure with them, also – in the prison vaults of Londra. Dorian Hawkmoon, Count Brass, the philosopher Bowgentle, the unhuman one, Oladahn of the Bulgar Mountains, and the traitor Huillam D'Averc – all these shall suffer for many years. That I have sworn by the Runestaff!"

There was a sound behind them. They turned to peer through the flickering light and saw a canopied litter being borne up the hill by a dozen Athenan prisoners of war who were chained to its poles. In the litter lounged the unconventional Shenegar Trott, Count of Sussex. Count Shenegar almost disdained the wearing of a mask at all, and as it was he wore a silver one scarcely larger than his head, fashioned to resemble, in caricature, his own visage. He belonged to no Order and was tolerated by the King-Emperor and his Court because of his immense richness and almost superhuman courage in battle – yet he gave the appearance, in his jeweled robes and lazy manner, of a besotted fool. He, even more than Meliadus, had the confidence (such as it was) of the King-Emperor Huon, for his advice was almost always excellent. He had plainly heard the last part of the exchange and spoke banteringly.

"A dangerous oath to swear, my lord Baron," said he softly. "One that could, by all counts, have repercussions on he who swears it . . ."

"I swore the oath with that knowledge," replied Meliadus. "I shall find them, Count Shenegar, never fear."

"I came to remind you, my lords," said Shenegar Trott, "that our King-Emperor grows impatient to see us and hear our report that all Europe is now his property."

"I will ride for Londra instantly," Meliadus said. "For there I may consult our sorcerer-scientists and discover a means of hunting out my foes. Farewell, my lords."

He dragged at his horse's reins, turning the beast and galloping back down the hill, watched by his peers.

The beast-masks moved together in the firelight. "His

11

singular mentality could destroy us all," whispered one.

"What matter?" chuckled Shenegar Trott, "so long as all is destroyed with us . . ."

The answering laughter was wild, ringing from the jeweled helms. It was insane laughter, tinged as much with self-hatred as with hatred of the world.

For this was the great power of the Lords of the Dark Empire, that they valued nothing on all the Earth, no human quality, nothing within or without themselves. The spreading of conquest and desolation, of terror and torment, was their staple entertainment, a means of employing their hours until their spans of life were ended. For them, warfare was merely the most satisfactory way of easing their ennui . . .

Chapter Two
THE FLAMINGOES DANCE

At dawn, when clouds of giant scarlet flamingoes rose from their nests of reeds and wheeled through the sky in bizarre ritual dances, Count Brass would stand on the edge of the marsh and stare over the water at the strange configurations of dark lagoons and tawny islands that seemed to him like hieroglyphs in some primeval language.

The ontological revelations that might exist in these patterns had always intrigued him, and of late he had taken to studying the birds, reeds and lagoons, attempting to divine the key to this cryptic landscape.

The landscape, he thought, was coded. In it he might find the answers to the dilemma of which even he was only half-conscious; find, perhaps, the revelation that would tell him what he needed to know of the growing threat he felt was about to engulf him both psychically and physically.

The sun rose, brightening the water with its pale light, and Count Brass heard a sound, turned, and saw his daughter Yisselda, golden-haired madonna of the lagoons, an almost preternatural figure in her flowing blue gown, riding bareback her white horned Kamarg horse and smiling mysteriously as if she, too, knew some secret that he could never fully comprehend.

Count Brass sought to avoid the girl by stepping out briskly along the shore, but already she was riding close to him and waving.

"Father – you're up early! Not for the first time recently."

Count Brass nodded, turned again to contemplate the waters and the reeds, looked up suddenly at the dancing birds as if to catch them by surprise, or by some instinctive flash of divination learn the secret of their strange, almost frenetic gyrations.

Yisselda had dismounted and now stood beside him. "They were not our flamingoes," she said. "And yet they're so like them. What do you see?"

Count Brass shrugged and smiled at her. "Nothing. Where's Hawkmoon?"

"At the castle. He's still asleep."

Count Brass grunted, clasping his great hands together as if in desperate prayer, listening to the beating of the heavy wings overhead. Then he relaxed and took her by the arm, guiding her along the bank of the lagoon.

"It's beautiful," she murmured. "The sunrise."

Count Brass made a small gesture of impatience. "You don't understand . . ." he began, and then paused. He knew that she would never see the landscape as he saw it. He had tried once to describe it to her, but she had lost interest quickly, had made no effort to see the significance of the patterns he saw everywhere – in the water, the reeds, the trees, the animal life that filled this Kamarg in abundance, as it had filled the Kamarg that they had left.

To him it was the quintessence of order, but to her it was simply pleasurable to look at – something "beautiful," to admire, in fact, for its "wildness."

Only Bowgentle, the philosopher poet, his old friend, had an inkling of what he meant and even then Bowgentle believed that it reflected not on the nature of the landscape but on the particular nature of Count Brass's mind.

"You're exhausted, disorientated," Bowgentle would say. "The ordering mechanism of the brain is working too hard, so you see a pattern to existence that, in fact, only stems from your

13

own weariness and disturbance . . ."

Count Brass would dismiss this argument with a scowl, don his armor of brass and ride away on his own again, to the discomfort of his family and friends. He had spent a long while exploring this new Kamarg that was so much like his own save that there was no evidence of mankind's ever having existed here.

"He is a man of action, like myself," Dorian Hawkmoon, Yisselda's husband, would say. "His mind turns inward, I fear, for want of some real problem with which to engage itself."

"The real problems seem insoluble," Bowgentle would reply, and the conversation would end as Hawkmoon, too, went off by himself, his hand on the hilt of his sword.

There was tension in Castle Brass, and even in the village below, the folk were troubled, glad of their escape from the terror of the Dark Empire, but not sure that they were permanently settled in this new land so like the one they had left. At first, when they had arrived, the land had seemed a transformed version of the Kamarg, its colors those of the rainbow, but gradually those colors had changed to more natural ones, as if their memories had imposed themselves on the landscape, so that now there was little difference. There were herds of horned horses and white bulls to tame, scarlet flamingoes that might be trained to bear riders, but at the back of the villagers' minds was always the threat of the Dark Empire somehow finding a way through even to this retreat.

To Hawkmoon and Count Brass – perhaps to D'Averc, Bowgentle and Oladahn, too – the idea was not so threatening. There were times when they would have welcomed an assault from the world they had left.

While Count Brass studied the landscape and sought to divine its secrets, Dorian Hawkmoon would ride at speed along the lagoon trails, scattering herds of bulls and horses, sending the flamingoes flapping into the sky, looking for an enemy.

One day, as he rode back on a steaming horse from one of his many journeys of exploration along the shores of the violet sea (sea and terrain seemed without limit), he saw the flamingoes wheeling in the sky, spiraling upwards on the air currents and then drifting down again. It was afternoon and the flamingo dance took place only at dawn. The giant birds seemed disturbed and Hawkmoon decided to investigate.

He spurred his horse along the winding path through the

14

marsh until he was directly below the flamingoes, saw that they wheeled above a small island covered in tall reeds. He peered intently at the island and thought that he glimpsed something among the reeds, a flash of red that could be a man's coat.

At first Hawkmoon decided that it was probably a villager snaring duck, but then he realised that if that had been so the man would have hailed him – at least waved him away so that he would not disturb the fowl.

Puzzled, Hawkmoon spurred his horse into the water, swimming it across to the island and on to the marshy ground. The animal's powerful body pushed back the tough reeds as it moved and again Hawkmoon saw a flash of red, became convinced that he had seen a man.

"Ho!" he cried. "Who's there!"

He received no answer. Instead the reeds became more agitated as the man began to run through them without caution.

"Who are you?" Hawkmoon cried, and it came to him then that the Dark Empire had broken through at last, that there were men hidden everywhere in the reeds ready to attack Castle Brass.

He thundered through the reeds in pursuit of the red-jerkined man, saw him clearly now as he flung himself into the lagoon and began to swim for the bank.

"Stop!" Hawkmoon called, but the man swam on.

Hawkmoon's horse plunged again into the water and it foamed white. The man was already wading onto the opposite bank, glanced back to see that Hawkmoon was almost upon him, turned right round and drew a bright, slender sword of extraordinary length.

But it was not the sword that astonished Hawkmoon most – it was the impression that the man had no face! The whole of the head beneath the long, fair, dirty hair was blank. Hawkmoon gasped, drawing his own sword. Was it some alien inhabitant of this world?

Hawkmoon swung himself from his saddle, sword ready, as the horse clambered onto the bank, stood legs astraddle facing his strange antagonist, laughed suddenly as he realized the truth. The man was wearing a mask of light leather. The mouth and eye slits were very thin and could not be distinguished at a distance.

"Why do you laugh?" the masked man asked in a braying

15

voice, his sword on guard. "You should not laugh, my friend, for you are about to die."

"Who are you?" Hawkmoon asked. "I know you for a boaster only."

"I am a greater swordsman than you," replied the man. "You had best surrender now."

"I regret I can't accept your word on the quality of my swordsmanship or your own," Hawkmoon replied with a smile. "How is it that such a master of the blade is so poorly attired, for instance?"

With his sword he indicated the man's patched red jerkin, his trousers and boots of cracked leather. Even his bright sword had no scabbard, but had been drawn from a loop of cord attached to a rope belt on which also dangled a purse that bulged. On the man's fingers were rings of obvious glass and paste and the flesh of his skin looked grey and unhealthy. The body was tall but stringy, half-starved by the look of it.

"A beggar, I'd guess," mocked Hawkmoon. "Where did you steal the sword, beggar?"

He gasped as the man thrust suddenly, then withdrew. The movement had been incredibly rapid and Hawkmoon felt a sting on his cheek, put up his hand to his face and discovered that it bled.

"Shall I prick you thus to death?" sneered the stranger. "Put down your heavy sword and make yourself my prisoner."

Hawkmoon laughed with real pleasure. "Good! A worthy opponent after all. You do not know how much I welcome you, my friend. It has been too long since I heard the ring of steel in my ears!" And with that he lunged at the masked man.

His adversary deftly defended himself with a parry that some-how became a thrust which Hawkmoon barely managed to block in time. Feet planted firmly in the marshy ground, neither moved an inch from his position, both fought skillfully and unheatedly, each recognising in the other a true master of the sword.

They fought for an hour, absolutely matched, neither giving nor sustaining a wound, and Hawkmoon decided on different tactics, began gradually to shift back down the bank towards the water.

Thinking that Hawkmoon was retreating, the masked man seemed to gain confidence and his sword moved even more rapidly than before so that Hawkmoon was forced to exert all his energy to deflect it.

Then Hawkmoon pretended to slip in the mud, going down on one knee. The other sprang forward to thrust and Hawkmoon's blade moved rapidly, the flat striking the man's wrist. He yelled and the sword fell from his hand. Quickly Hawkmoon jumped up and placed his boot upon the weapon, his blade at the other's throat.

"Not a trick worthy of a true swordsman," grumbled the masked man.

"I am easily bored," Hawkmoon replied. "I was becoming impatient with the game."

"Well, what now?"

"Your name?" Hawkmoon said. "I'll know that first – then see your face – then know your business here – then, and perhaps most important, discover how you came here."

"My name you will know," said the man with undisguised pride. "It is Elvereza Tozer."

"I do know it, indeed!" remarked the Duke of Köln in some surprise.

Chapter Three
ELVEREZA TOZER

ELVEREZA TOZER was not the man Hawkmoon would have expected to meet if he had been told in advance that he was to encounter Granbretan's greatest playwright – a writer whose work was admired throughout Europe, even by those who in all other ways loathed Granbretan. The author of *King Staleen*, *The Tragedy of Katine and Carna*, *The Last of the Braldurs*, *Annala*, *Chirshil and Adulf*, *The Comedy of Steel* and many more, had not been heard of of late, but Hawkmoon had thought this due to the wars. He would have expected Tozer to have been rich in dress, confident in every way, poised and full of wit. Instead he found a man who seemed more at ease with a

17

sword than with words, a vain man, something of a fool and a poppinjay, dressed in rags.

As he propelled Tozer with his own sword along the marsh trails towards Castle Brass, Hawkmoon puzzled over this apparent paradox. Was the man lying? If so, why should he claim to be, of all things, an eminent playmaker?

Tozer walked along, apparently undisturbed by his change of fortune, whistling a jaunty tune.

Hawkmoon paused. "A moment," he said, and reached to grasp the reins of his horse, which had been following him. Tozer turned. He still wore his mask. Hawkmoon had been so astonished at hearing the name that he had forgotten to order Tozer to remove the leather from his face.

"Well," Tozer said, glancing about him. "It is a lovely country – though short in audiences, I would gather."

"Aye," replied Hawkmoon, nonplussed. "Aye . . ." He gestured towards the horse. "We'll ride pillion, I think. Into the saddle with you, Master Tozer."

Tozer swung up onto the horse and Hawkmoon followed him, taking the reins and urging the horse into a trot.

In this manner they rode until they came to the gates of the town, passed through them, and proceeded slowly through the winding streets, up the steep road to the walls of Castle Brass.

Dismounting in the courtyard, Hawkmoon gave the horse to a groom and indicated the door to the main hall of the castle. "Through there, if you please," he told Tozer.

With a small shrug, Tozer sauntered through the door and bowed to the two men who stood there by the great fire which blazed in the hall. Hawkmoon nodded to them. "Good morning, Sir Bowgentle – D'Averc. I have a prisoner . . ."

"So I see," D'Averc said, his gaunt, handsome features brightening a little with interest. "Are the warriors of Granbretan at our gates again?"

"He is the only one, so far as I can judge," Hawkmoon replied. "He claims to be Elvereza Tozer . . ."

"Indeed?" The ascetic Bowgentle's quiet eyes took on a look of curiosity. "The author of *Chirshil and Adulf*? It is hard to believe."

Tozer's thin hand went to the mask and tugged at the thongs securing it. "I know you, sir," he said. "We met ten years hence when I came with my play to Malaga."

18

"I recall the time. We discussed some poems you had recently published and which I admired." Bowgentle shook his head. "You *are* Elvereza Tozer, but . . ."

The mask came loose and revealed an emaciated, shifty face sporting a whispy beard which did not hide a weak, receding chin and which was dominated by a long, thin nose. The flesh of the face was unhealthy and bore the marks of a pox.

"And I recall the face – though it was fuller then. Pray, what has happened to you, sir ?" Bowgentle asked faintly. "Are you a refugee seeking escape from your countrymen ?"

"Ah," Tozer sighed, darting Bowgentle a calculating look. "Perhaps. Would you have a glass of wine, sir ? My encounter with your military friend here has left me thirsty, I fear."

"What ?" put in D'Averc. "Have you been fighting ?"

"Fighting to kill," Hawkmoon said grimly. "I feel that Master Tozer did not come to our Kamarg on an errand of goodwill. I found him skulking in the reeds to the south. I think he comes as a spy."

"And why should Elvereza Tozer, greatest playwright of the world, wish to *spy* ?" The words were delivered by Tozer in a disdainful tone that yet somehow lacked conviction

Bowgentle bit his lip and tugged a bell rope for a servant.

"That is for you to tell us, sir," Huillam D'Averc said with some amusement in his voice. He coughed ostentatiously. "Forgive me – a slight chill, I think. The castle is full of drafts . . ."

"And I'd wish the same for myself," Tozer said, "If a *draft* could be found." He looked at them expectantly. "A draft to help us forget the draft, if you understand me. A draft . . ."

"Yes, yes," said Bowgentle hastily and turned to the servant who had entered. "A jug of wine for our guest," he requested. "And would you eat, Master Tozer ?"

" 'I would eat the bread of Babel and the meat of Marakhan . . .' ", Tozer said dreamily. " 'For all such fruits as fools supply are merely . . .' "

"We can offer some cheese at this hour," D'Averc interrupted sardonically.

"*Annala*, Act VI, Scene V," Tozer said. "You'll remember the scene ?"

"I remember," D'Averc nodded. "I always felt that section somewhat weaker than the rest."

"Subtler," Tozer said airily. "Subtler."

The servant re-entered with the wine and Tozer helped himself, pouring a generous amount into the goblet. "The concerns of literature," he said, "are not always obvious to the common herd. A hundred years from now and people will see the last act of *Annala* not, as some stupid critics have said, as hastily written and poorly conceived, but as the complex structure it really is . . ."

"I had reckoned myself as something of a writer," Bowgentle said, "but I must confess, I did not see subtleties . . . Perhaps you could explain."

"Some other time," Tozer told him, with an insouciant wave of the hand. He drank off the wine and helped himself to another full goblet.

"In the meanwhile," Hawkmoon said firmly, "perhaps you could explain your presence in the Kamarg. After all, we had thought ourselves inviolate and now . . ."

"You are still inviolate, never fear," Tozer said, "save to myself, of course. By the power of my brain I propelled myself hither."

D'Averc sceptically rubbed his chin. "By the power of your – *brain*? How so?"

"An ancient discipline taught me by a master philosopher who dwells in the hidden valleys of Yel . . ." Tozer belched and poured more wine.

"Yel is that south western province of Granbretan is it not?" Bowgentle asked.

"Aye. A remote, barely inhabited land, peopled by a few dark-brown barbarians who live in holes in the ground. After my play *Chirshil and Adulf* had incurred the displeasure of certain elements at Court, I deemed it wise to retire there for a while, leaving my enemies to take for themselves all goods, monies, and mistresses I left behind. What know I of petty politics? How was I to realise that certain portions of the play seemed to reflect the intrigues then current at the Court?"

"So you were disgraced?" Hawkmoon said, looking narrowly at Tozer. The story could be part of the man's deception.

"More – I almost lost my life. But the rural existence near killed me as it was . . ."

"You met this philosopher who taught you how to travel

through the dimensions? Then you came here seeking refuge?"
Hawkmoon studied Tozer's reaction to these questions.

"No – ah, yes . . ." said the playwright. "That is to say, I did not know exactly where I was coming . . ."

"I think that you were sent here by the King-Emperor to destroy us," Hawkmoon said. "I think, Master Tozer, that you are lying to us."

"Lying? What is a lie? What is truth?" Tozer grinned glassily up at Hawkmoon and then hiccuped.

"Truth," Hawkmoon replied evenly, "is a coarse noose about your throat. I think we should hang you." He fingered the dull black jewels imbedded in his forehead. "I am not unfamiliar with the tricks of the Dark Empire. I have been their victim too often to risk being deceived again." He looked at the others. "I say we should hang him now."

"But how do we know if he is really the only one who can reach us?" D'Averc asked sensibly. "We cannot be too hasty, Hawkmoon."

"I am the only one, I swear it!" Tozer spoke nervously now. "I admit, good sir, that I was commissioned to come here. It was that or lose my life in the prison catacombs of the Great Palace. When I had the old man's secret, I returned to Londra thinking that my power would enable me to bargain with those at Court who were displeased with me. I wished only to be returned to my former status and know that I had an audience to write for once again. However, when I told them of my new-found discipline, they instantly threatened my life unless I came here and destroyed that which enabled you to enter this dimension . . . so I came – glad, I must admit, to escape them. I was not particularly willing to risk my skin in offending you good folk but . . ."

"They did not ensure, in some way, that you would perform the task they set you?" Hawkmoon asked. "That is strange."

"To tell you the truth," Tozer said, downcast, "I do not think they altogether believed in my power. I think they merely wished to test that I had it. When I agreed to go and left instantly, they must have been shocked."

"Not like the Dark Empire Lords to make such an oversight," mused D'Averc, his aquiline face frowning. "Still, if you did not win our confidence, there's no reason you should have won theirs. Nonetheless, I am not altogether convinced that you

21

speak the truth."

"You told them of this old man?" Bowgentle said. "They will be able to learn his secret for themselves!"

"Not so," Tozer said with a leer. "I told them I had struck upon the power myself, in my months of solitude."

"No wonder they did not take you seriously," D'Averc smiled.

Tozer looked hurt and took another draft of wine.

"I find it difficult to believe that you were able to travel here by exercise of your will alone," Bowgentle admitted. "Are you sure you employed no other means . . . ?"

"None."

"I like this not at all," Hawkmoon said darkly. "Even if he tells the truth, the Lords of Granbretan will wonder where he found his power by now, will learn all his movements, will almost certainly discover the old man – and then they will have the means to come through in strength and we shall be doomed!'

"Indeed, these are difficult times," Tozer said, filling his goblet yet again. "Remember your *King Staleen*, Act IV, Scene II – 'Wild days, wild riders, and the stink of warfare across the world!' Aha, I was a visionary and knew it not!" He was now evidently drunk.

Hawkmoon stared hard at the weak-chinned drunkard, still finding it almost impossible to believe that this was the great playwright Tozer.

"You wonder at my poverty, I see," Tozer said speaking with slurred tongue. "The result of a couple of lines in *Chirshil and Adulf*, as I told you. Oh, the wickedness of fate! A couple of lines, penned in good faith, and here I am today, with the threat of a noose about my gullet. You remember the scene of course, and the speech? 'Court and king, alike corrupt . . . ?' Act I, Scene I? Pity me, sir, and do not hang me. A great artist destroyed by his own mighty genius."

"This old man," Bowgentle said. "What was he like? Where exactly did he live?"

"The old man . . ." Tozer forced more wine down his throat. "The old man reminded me somewhat of Ioni in my *Comedy of Steel*. Act II, Scene VI . . ."

"What was he like?" Hawkmoon asked impatiently.

" 'Machine-devoured, all his hours were given o'er to that insidious circuitry, and old grew he, unnoticing, in the service

22

of his engines.' He lived only for his science, you see. He made the rings . . ." Tozer put his hand to his mouth.

"Rings? What rings?" D'Averc said swiftly.

"I feel that you must excuse me," Tozer said, rising in a parody of dignity, "for the wine has proved too rich for my empty stomach. Your pity, if you please . . ."

It was true that Tozer's face had taken on a greenish tinge.

"Very well," Bowgentle said wearily. "I will show you."

"Before he leaves," came a new voice from near the door, "ask him for the ring he wears on the middle finger of his left hand." The tone was slightly muffled, a little sardonic. Hawkmoon recognized it at once and turned.

Tozer gasped and clamped his hand over the ring.

"What do you know of this?" he said. "Who are you?"

"Duke Dorian here," said the figure with a gesture towards Hawkmoon, "calls me the warrior in Jet and Gold."

Taller than any of them, covered all in armor and helm of black and gold, the mysterious Warrior raised an arm and pointed a metal-clad finger at Tozer. "Hand him that ring."

"The ring is of glass, nothing more. It is of no value . . ."

D'Averc said. "He mentioned rings. Is the ring, then, what actually transported him here?"

Tozer still hesitated, his face stupid with drink and with anxiety. "I said that it was glass, of no value . . ."

"By the Runestaff, I command thee!" rumbled the Warrior in a terrible voice.

With a little nervous movement. Elvereza Tozer drew off the ring and flung it onto the flagstones. D'Averc stooped and caught it up, inspecting it. "It's a crystal," he said, "not glass. A familiar kind of crystal, too . . ."

"It is of the same substance from which the device that brought you here was carved," the Warrior in Jet and Gold told him. He displayed his own gauntleted hand and there, on the middle finger, reposed an identical ring. "And it possesses the same properties – can transport a man through the dimensions.'

"As I thought," Hawkmoon said. "It was no mental discipline that enabled you to come here, but a piece of crystal. Now I'll hang you assuredly! Where did you get the ring?"

"From the man – from Mygan of Llandar. I swear that is the truth. He has others – can make more!" Tozer cried. "Do not hang me, I pray you. I will tell you exactly where to find the old man."

"That we shall have to know," Bowgentle said thoughtfully, "for we shall have to get to him before the Dark Empire Lords do. We must have him and his secrets – for our security."

"What? Must we journey to Granbretan?" D'Averc said in some astonishment.

"It would seem necessary," Hawkmoon told him.

Chapter Four
FLANA MIKOSEVAAR

AT THE CONCERT, Flana Mikosevaar, Countess of Kanbery, adjusted her mask of spun gold and glanced absently about her, seeing the rest of the audience only as a mass of gorgeous colours. The orchestra in the center of the ballroom played a wild and complex melody, one of the later works of Granbretan's last great musician, Londen Johne, who had died two centuries earlier.

The Countess's mask was that of an ornate heron, its eyes facetted with a thousand fragments of rare jewels. Her heavy gown was of luminous brocade that changed its many colors as the light varied. She was Asrovak Mikosevaar's widow, he who had died under Dorian Hawkmoon's blade at the first Battle of the Kamarg. The Muskovian renegade, who had formed the Vulture Legion to fight on the European mainland and whose slogan had been *Death to Life*, was not mourned by Flana of Kanbery and she bore no grudge against his killer. He had been her twelfth husband, after all, and the fierce insanity of the bloodlover had served her pleasure enough long before he set off to make war on the Kamarg. Since then she had had several lovers and her memory of Asrovak Mikosevaar was as cloudy as all her other memories of men, for Flana was an inturned creature who barely distinguished between one person and another.

It was her habit, on the whole, to have husbands and lovers destroyed when they became inconvenient to her. An instinct, rather than any intellectual consideration, stopped her from murdering the more powerful ones. This was not to say that she was incapable of love, for she could love passionately, doting entirely on the object of her love, but she could not sustain the emotion for long. Hatred was unknown to her, as was loyalty. She was for the most part a neutral animal, reminding some of a cat and others of a spider – though in her grace and beauty she was more reminiscent of the former. And there were many who bore her hatred, who planned vengeance against her for a husband stolen or a brother poisoned, who would have taken that vengeance had she not been the Countess of Kanbery and cousin to the King-Emperor Huon, that immortal monarch who dwelt eternally in his womblike Throne Globe in the huge throne room of his palace. She was the center of other attentions, also, since she was the only surviving kin of the monarch, and certain elements at court considered that with Huon destroyed she could be made Queen-Empress and serve their interests.

Unaware of any plots concerning her, Flana of Kanbery would have been unperturbed had she been told of them, for she had not the faintest curiosity about the affairs of any one of her species, sought only to satisfy her own obscure desires, to ease the strange, melancholy longing in her soul which she could not define. Many had wondered about her, sought her favors with the sole object of unmasking her to see what they could learn in her face, but her face, fair-skinned, beautiful, the cheeks slightly flushed always, the eyes large and golden, held a look remote and mysterious, hiding far more than could any golden mask.

The music ceased, the audience moved, and the colors became alive as the fabrics swirled and masks turned, nodded, gestured. The delicate masks of the ladies could be seen gathering around the warlike helms of those recently returned captains of Granbretan's great armies. The Countess rose but did not move towards them. Vaguely she recognised some of the helms – particularly that of Meliadus of the Wolf Order, who had been her husband five years earlier and who had divorced her (an action she had hardly noticed). There, too, was Shenegar Trott, lounging on heaped cushions, served by naked mainland slavegirls, his silver mask a parody of a human face. And she saw the mask of the Duke of Lakasdeh, Pra Flenn, barely eighteen and with ten great cities fallen to him. his helm a grinning dragon head. The others she thought she knew, and she understood that they were all the mightiest warlords, back to celebrate their victories, to divide up the conquered territories between them, to receive the congratulations of their Emperor. They laughed considerably, stood proudly as the ladies flattered them, all but her ex-husband Meliadus, who appeared to avoid them and conferred instead with his brother-in-law Taragorm, Master of the Palace of Time, and the serpent-masked Baron Kalan of Vitall, Grand Constable of the Order of the Snake and chief scientist to the King-Emperor. Behind her mask, Flana frowned, remembering distantly that Meliadus normally avoided Taragorm . . .

Chapter Five
TARAGORM

"AND HOW HAVE you fared, Brother Taragorm?" asked Meliadus with forced cordiality.

The man who had married his sister replied shortly: "Well." He wondered why Meliadus should approach him thus when it was well known that Meliadus was profoundly jealous of Taragorm's having won his sister's affections. The huge mask lifted a little superciliously. It was constructed of a monstrous clock of gilded and enameled brass, with numerals of inlaid mother-o'-pearl and hands of filligree'd silver, the box in which hung its pendulum extending to the upper part of Taragorm's broad chest. The box was of some transparent material, like glass of a bluish tint, and through it could be seen the golden pendulum swinging back and forth. The whole clock was balanced by means of a complex mechanism so as to adjust to Taragorm's every movement. It struck the hour, half-hour and quarter-hour and at midday and midnight chimed the first eight bars of Sheneven's *Temporal Antipathies*.

"And how," continued Meliadus in this same unusually

ingratiating manner, "do the clocks of your palace fare? All the ticks ticking and the tocks tocking, mmm?"

It took Taragorm a moment to understand that his brother-in-law was, in fact, attempting to joke. He made no reply.

Meliadus cleared his throat.

Kalan of the serpent mask said: "I hear you are experimenting with some machine capable of travelling through time, Lord Taragorm. As it happens, I, too, have been experimenting – with an engine . . ."

"I wished to ask you, brother, about your experiments," Meliadus said to Taragorm. "How far advanced are they?"

"Reasonably advanced, brother."

"You have moved through time already?"

"Not personally."

"My engine," Baron Kalan continued implacably, "is capable of moving ships at enormous speeds across vast distances. Why, we could invade any land on the globe, no matter how far away . . ."

"When will the point be reached," Meliadus asked moving closer to Taragorm, "when a man can journey into the past or future?"

Baron Kalan shrugged and turned away. "I must return to my laboratories," he said. "The King-Emperor has commissioned me urgently to complete my work. Good day, my lords."

"Good day," said Meliadus absently. "Now, brother, you must tell me more of your work – show me, perhaps, how far you have progressed."

"I must," Taragorm replied facetiously. "But my work is secret, brother. I cannot take you to the Palace of Time without the permission of King Huon. That you must seek first."

"Surely unnecessary for me to seek such permission?"

"None is so great that he can act without the blessing of our King-Emperor."

"But the matter is of extraordinary importance, brother," Meliadus said, his tone almost desperate, almost wheedling. "Our enemies have escaped us, probably to another era of the Earth, from what I can gather. They offer a threat to Granbretan's security!"

"You speak of that handful of ruffians whom you failed to defeat at the Battle of the Kamarg?"

"They were almost conquered – only science or sorcery saved

27

them from our vengeance. No one blames me for my failure . . ."

"Save yourself? You do not blame yourself?"

"No blame to me, at all, from any quarter. I would finish the matter, that's all. I would rid the Empire of her enemies. Where's the fault in that?"

"I have heard it whispered that your battle is more private than public, that you have made foolish compromises in order to pursue a personal vendetta against those who dwell in the Kamarg."

"That is an opinion, brother," Meliadus said, restraining with difficulty his chagrin. "But I fear only for our Empire's well-being."

"Then tell King Huon of this fear and he may then permit you to visit my palace." Taragorm turned away, as he did so his mask beginning to boom out the hour, making any further conversation momentarily impossible. Meliadus made to follow him, then changed his mind, walking, fuming, from the hall.

Surrounded now by young lords, each seeking to attract her deadly attentions, Countess Flana Mikosevaar watched Baron Meliadus depart.

By the impatient manner of his gait, she assumed him to be in uneven temper. Then she forgot him as she returned her attention to the flatteries of her attendants, listening not to the words (which were familiar to her) but to the voices themselves which were like old, favorite tunes.

Taragorm, now, was conversing with Shenegar Trott.

"I am to present myself to the King-Emperor in the morning,' Trott told the Master of the Palace of Time. "Some commission, I believe, that is at this moment a secret known only to himself. We must keep busy, Lord Taragorm, eh?"

"Indeed, we must, Count Shenegar, lest boredom engulfs us all."

Chapter Six
THE AUDIENCE

NEXT MORNING Meliadus waited impatiently outside the King-Emperor's throne room. He had requested an audience the previous evening and had been told to present himself at eleven o'clock. It was now twelve and the doors had not yet opened to admit him. The doors, towering into the dimness of the huge roof, were encrusted with jewels that made up a mosaic of images of ancient things. The fifty mantis-masked guards who blocked them, stood stock still with flame-lances ready at a precise angle. Meliadus strode up and down before them; behind him, the glittering corridors of the King Emperor's hallucinatory palace.

Meliadus attempted to fight back his feelings of resentment that the King Emperor had not granted him an immediate audience. After all, was he not paramount Warlord of Europe? Had it not been under his direction that the armies of Granbretan had conquered a continent? Had he not taken those same armies into the Middle East and added further territories to the domain of the Dark Empire? Why should the King-Emperor seek to insult him in this manner? Meliadus, first of Granbretan's warriors, should have priority over all lesser mortals. He suspected a plot against him. From what Taragorm and the others had said, they judged him to be losing his grip. They were fools if they did not realise the threat that Hawkmoon, Count Brass and Huillam D'Averc offered. Let them escape their deserved reckoning and it would inflame others to rebel, make the work of conquest less speedy. Surely King Huon had not listened to those who spoke against him? The King Emperor was wise, the King Emperor was objective. If he were not, then he was unfit to rule . . .

Meliadus dismissed the thought in horror.

At last the jewelled doors began to move open until they were

29

wide enough to admit a single man – and through this crack strode a jaunty, corpulent figure.

"Shenegar Trott!" exclaimed Meliadus. "Is it you who has kept me waiting so long?"

Trott's silver mask glinted in the light from the corridors. "My apologies, Baron Meliadus. My deep apologies. There were many details to discuss. But I am finished now. A mission, my dear Baron – I have a mission! Such a mission, ha, ha!"

And before Meliadus could tax him further on the nature of his mission, he had swept away.

From within the Throne Room now issued a youthful, vibrant voice, the voice of the King Emperor himself.

"You may join me now, Baron Meliadus."

The mantis warriors parted their ranks and allowed the baron to pass through them and into the Throne Room.

Into that gigantic hall of blazing color, where hung the bright banners of Granbretan's five hundred noblest families, which was lined on either side by a thousand statue-still mantis guards, stepped Baron Meliadus of Kroiden and abased himself.

Ornate gallery upon ornate gallery stretched upwards and upwards to the concave ceiling of the hall. The armor of the soldiers of the Order of the Mantis shone black and green and gold, and in the distance, as he rose to his feet, Baron Meliadus saw his King Emperor's Throne Globe, a white speck against the green and purple of the walls behind it.

Walking slowly, it took Meliadus twenty minutes to reach the globe and once again abase himself. The globe contained a sluggishly swirling liquid that was milk-white but which was sometimes streaked with iridescent veins of blood-red and blue. At the center of this fluid was curled King Huon himself, a wrinkled, ancient foetus-like creature that was immortal and in which the only things that seemed alive were the eyes, black, sharp and malicious.

"Baron Meliadus," came the golden voice that had been torn from the throat of a beautiful youth to furnish King Huon with speech.

"Great Majesty," murmured Meliadus. "I thank you for your graciousness in permitting this audience."

"And for what purpose did you desire the audience, baron?"

The tone was sardonic, a trifle impatient. "Do you seek to hear us praise again your efforts on our behalf in Europe?"

"The accomplishment is enough, noble sire. I seek to warn you that danger still threatens us in Europe . . ."

"What? You have not made the continent wholly ours?"

"You know that I have, Great Emperor, from one coast to the other, to the very borders of Muskovia and beyond. Few live who are not totally our slaves. But I refer to those who fled us . . ."

"Hawkmoon and his friends?"

"The same, Mighty King Emperor."

"You chased them away. They offer us no threat."

"While they live, they threaten us, noble sire, for their escape could give others hope, and hope we must destroy in all we conquer lest we are troubled by risings against your discipline."

"You have dealt with risings before. You are used to them. We fear, Baron Meliadus, that you may be forsaking your King Emperor's interests in favor of personal interests . . ."

"My personal interests are your interests, Great King Emperor, your interests are my personal interests – they are indivisible. Am I not the most loyal of your servants?"

"Perhaps you believe yourself to be, Baron Meliadus, perhaps you believe yourself to be . . ."

"What do you mean, Powerful Monarch?"

"We mean that your obsession with the German Hawkmoon and that handful of villains he has as friends could not necessarily be in our interest. They will not return – and if they should dare return, why, we can deal with them then. We fear that it is vengeance alone which motivates you and that you have rationalised your thirst for vengeance into a belief that the whole Dark Empire is threatened by those you would be avenged upon."

"No! No, Prince of All! I swear that is not so!"

"Let them stay where they are, Meliadus. Deal with them only if they reappear."

"Great King, they offer a potential threat to the Empire. There are other powers involved who support them – else where could they have obtained the machine which plucked them away when we were about to destroy them? I cannot offer positive evidence now – but if you would let me work with Taragorm to use his knowledge to discover the whereabouts of Hawkmoon and his company – then I will find that evidence and you will believe me!"

"We are dubious, Meliadus, we are dubious." There was a grim note now in the melodious voice. "But if it does not interfere with the other duties at court that we intend to give you, you may visit Lord Taragorm's palace and seek his assistance in your attempts to locate your enemies . . ."

"Our enemies, Prince of All . . ."

"We shall see, baron, we shall see."

"I thank you for your faith in me, Great Majesty. I will – "

"The audience is not ended, Baron Meliadus, for we have not yet told you of those duties at court we mentioned."

"I shall be honoured to perform them, noble sire."

"You spoke of our security being in peril from the Kamarg. Well, we believe that we may be threatened from other quarters. To be precise we are anxious that the East may promise us a fresh enemy that could be, from what we gather, as powerful as the Dark Empire itself. Now, this could have something to do with your own suspicions concerning Hawkmoon and his supposed allies, for it is possible that we entertain representatives of those allies this day at our court . . ."

"Great King Emperor, if that be so . . ."

"Let us continue, Baron Meliadus!"

"I apologize, noble sire."

"Last night there appeared at the gates of Londra two strangers who claimed to be emissaries from the Empire of Asiacommunista. Their arrival was mysterious – indicating to us that they have methods of transport unknown to us, for they told us they had left their capital not two hours before. It is our opinion that they have come here, as we would visit others in whose territories we were interested, to spy out our strength. We, in turn, must try to gauge *their* power, for the time must come, even if it is not soon, when we shall be in conflict with them. Doubtless our conquests in the Near and Middle East have become known to them and they are nervous. We must discover all we can about them, try to convince them that we mean them no harm, try to persuade them to let us return emissaries to their domain. Should that prove possible, we should want you, Meliadus, to be one of those emissaries, for you have greater experience of such diplomacy than any other among our servants."

32

"This is disturbing news, Great Emperor."

"Aye, but we must take what advantage we can from the events. You will be their guide, treat them courteously, try to bring them out, make them expand upon the extent of their power and the size of their territories, the number of warriors their monarch commands, the power of their weaponry and the capabilities of their transports. This visit, Baron Meliadus, offers, as you can see, a much more important potential threat than any which may come from the vanished castle of Count Brass."

"Perhaps, noble sire . . ."

"No – certainly, Baron Meliadus!" The prehensible tongue flickered from the wrinkled mouth. "That is to be your most important task. If you have any time to spare, that can be devoted to your vendetta against Dorian Hawkmoon and the rest."

"But, Mighty King Emperor . . ."

"Bide our instructions well, Meliadus. Do not disappoint us." The tone was one of menace. The tongue touched the tiny jewel that floated near the head and the globe began to dull until it had the appearance of a solid, black sphere.

Chapter Seven
THE EMISSARIES

BARON MELIADUS COULD still not rid himself of the feeling that his King Emperor had lost his trust in him, that King Huon was deliberately finding means of curtailing his own schemes regarding the inhabitants of Castle Brass. True the king had made a convincing case for Meliadus's need to involve himself with the strange emissaries from Asiacommunista, had even flattered him by hinting that only Meliadus could deal with the problem, and would have the opportunity, later, of becoming not only the First Warrior of Europe, but also Paramount Warlord of Asiacommunista. But Meliadus's interest in Asiacommunista was not as great as his interest in Castle Brass –

for he felt that there was evidence for believing Castle Brass to be a considerable threat to the Dark Empire, whereas his monarch had no evidence to suppose that Asiacommunista threatened them.

Clad in his finest mask and most sumptuous garments, Meliadus made his way through the shining corridors of the palace towards the hall where the previous day he had sought out his brother-in-law Taragorm. Now the hall was to be used for another reception – to welcome, with due ceremony, the visitors from the east.

As the King Emperor's deputy, Baron Meliadus should have considered himself fully honored, for it gave him prestige second only to King Huon's, but even this knowledge did not entirely ease his vengeful mind.

He entered the hall to the sound of fanfares from the galleries that ran around the walls. All the noblest of Granbretan were assembled here, their finery splendid and dazzling. The emissaries from Asiacommunista had not yet been announced. Baron Meliadus walked to the dais on which were placed three golden thrones, mounted the steps and seated himself on the throne in the middle. The sea of nobles bowed before him and the hall was silent in anticipation. Meliadus himself had not yet met the emissaries. Captain Viel Phong of the Order of the Mantis had been their escort up to now.

Meliadus looked about the hall, noting the presence of Taragorm, of Flana, Countess of Kanbery, of Adaz Promp and Mygel Holst, of Jerek Nankenseen and Brenal Farnu. He was puzzled for a moment, wondering what was wrong. Then he realised that of all the great warrior nobles, only Shenegar Trott was missing. He remembered that the fat count had spoken of a mission. Had he left to fulfill it already? Why had not he, Meliadus, been informed of Trott's expedition? Were they keeping secrets from him? Had he truly lost the trust of his King Emperor? His brain in turmoil, Meliadus turned as the fanfares sounded again and the doors of the hall opened to admit two incredibly garbed figures.

Automatically Meliadus rose to greet them, astonished at the sight of them, for they were barbaric and grotesque – giants of over seven feet high, walking stiffly like automatons. Were they, indeed, human? he wondered. It had not occurred to him that they would not be. Were these some monstrous creation of the Tragic Millenium? Were the folk of Asiacommunista not men at all?

Like the people of Granbretan, they wore masks (he assumed those constructions on their shoulders were masks) so that it was impossible to tell if human faces were within them. They were tall things, roughly oblong in shape, of brightly painted leather in blues, greens, yellows and reds, swirling patterns on which had been painted devil features – glaring eyes and teeth-filled mouths. Bulky fur cloaks hung to the ground and the clothes they wore also seemed of leather, also painted to travesty human limbs and organs, reminding Meliadus of the colored sketches he had once seen in a medical text.

The herald announced them:

"The Lord Kominsar Kaow Shalang Gatt, Hereditary Representative of the President Emperor Jong Mang Shen of Asiacommunista and Prince Elect of the Hordes of the Sun."

The first of the emissaries stepped forward, his fur cloak drifting back to reveal shoulders that were at least four feet in width, the sleeves of his coat of bulky multi-colored silk, his right hand holding a staff of gem-encrusted gold that might have been the Runestaff itself, the care he took of it.

"The Lord Kominsar Orkai Heong Phoon, Hereditary Representative of the President Emperor Jong Mang Shen of Asiacommunista and Prince Elect of the Hordes of the Sun."

The second man (if man he was) stepped forward, similarly garbed but without a staff.

"I welcome the noble emissaries of the President Emperor Jong Mang Shen and let them know that all Granbretan is at their disposal to do with as they wish." Meliadus spread his arms wide.

The man with the staff paused before the dais and began to speak in a strange, lilting accent as if the language of Granbretan, and indeed all Europe and the Near East, was not native to him.

"We thank you most graciously for your welcome and would beg to know what mighty man addresses us."

"I am the Baron Meliadus of Kroiden, Grand Constable of the Order of the Wolf, Paramount Warlord of Europe, Deputy to the Immortal King Emperor Huon the Eighteenth, Ruler of Granbretan, of Europe and all the Realms of the Middle Sea, Grand Constable of the Order of the Mantis, Controller of

Destinies, Molder of Histories, Feared and Powerful Prince of All. I greet you as he would greet you, speak as he would speak, act in accord with all his wishes, for you must know that, being immortal, he cannot leave the mystic Throne Globe which preserves him and which is protected by the Thousand who guard him night and day." Meliadus thought it best to dwell for a moment upon the unvulnerability of the King Emperor, to impress the visitors, should it have occurred to them, that an attempt on King Huon's life was impossible. Meliadus indicated the twin thrones on either side of him. "I ask you – be seated, be entertained."

The two grotesque creatures mounted the steps and, with some difficulty, placed themselves in the golden chairs. There would be no banquet, for the people of Granbretan regarded eating, on the whole, as a personal matter, for it could necessitate the removal of their masks and the horror of displaying their naked faces. Only thrice a year did they shed in public their masks and garments in the security of the Throne Room itself where they would indulge in a week-long orgy before the greedy eyes of King Huon, taking part in disgusting and bloody ceremonies with names existing only in the languages of their various Orders and which were never referred to save upon those three occasions.

Baron Meliadus clapped his hands for the entertainments to begin, the courtiers parted like a curtain and took their places on the two sides of the hall, then on came the acrobats and the tumblers and the clowns while wild music sounded from the gallery above. Human pyramids swayed, bent and suddenly collapsed to reform again in even more complex assemblages, clowns capered and played upon one another the dangerous jokes that were expected of them, while the acrobats and tumblers cavorted around them at incredible speeds, walking on wires stretched between the galleries, performing on trapezes suspended high above all the heads of the audience.

Flana of Kanbery did not watch the tumblers and failed to see any humour in the actions of the clowns. Instead she turned her beautiful heron mask in the direction of the strangers and regarded them with what was for her unusual curiosity, thinking dimly that she would like to know them better, for they offered the possibility of a unique diversion, particularly if, as she suspected, they were not entirely manlike.

36

Meliadus, who could not rid the thought from his mind that he was being prejudiced against by his king and plotted against by his fellow nobles, made a mighty attempt to be civil to the visitors. When he wished, he could impress strangers (as he had once impressed Count Brass) with his dignity, his wit and his manliness, but this night it was an effort and he feared that the effort could be noticed in his tone.

"Do you find the entertainment to your liking, my lords of Asiacommunista?" he would say – and be met with a slight inclination of the huge heads. "Are the clowns not amusing?" – and there would be a movement of the hand from Kaow Shalang Gatt, who bore the golden staff – or: "Such skill! We brought those conjurers from our territories in Italia – and those tumblers were once the property of a Duke of Krahkov – you must have entertainers of equal skill at your own Emperor's court . . ." and the other, called Orkai Heong Phoon, would move his body in its seat, as if in discomfort. The result was to increase Baron Meliadus's sense of impatience, make him feel that these peculiar creatures somehow felt themselves above him or were bored by his attempts at civility and it became more and more difficult for him to continue the light conversation that was the only conversation possible while the music played.

At length he rose and clapped his hands. "Enough of this. Dismiss these entertainers. Let us have more exotic sport." And he relaxed a trifle as the sexual gymnasts entered the hall and began to perform for the delight of the depraved appetites of the Dark Empire. He chuckled, recognizing some of the performers, pointing them out to his guests. "There's one who was a Prince of Magyaria – and those two, the twins, were the sisters of a king in Turkia. I captured the blonde one there myself – and the stallion you see – in a Bulgarian stable. Many of them I personally trained." But though the entertainment relaxed the tortured nerves of Baron Meliadus of Kroiden, the emissaries of the President Emperor Jong Mang Shen seemed as unmoved and as taciturn as ever.

At last the performance was over and the entertainers retired (to the emissaries' relief, it seemed). Baron Meliadus, much refreshed, wondering if the creatures were of flesh and blood at all, gave the order for the ball to commence.

"Now gentlemen," said he rising, "shall we circulate about the floor so that you may meet those who have assembled to honor you and be honored by you."

Moving stiffly, the emissaries of Asiacommunista followed
Baron Meliadus, towering over the heads of even the tallest in
the hall.

"Would you dance?" asked the baron.

"We do not dance, I regret," said Kaow Shalang Gatt tone-
lessly, and since etiquette demanded that the guests dance
before the others could, no dancing was done. Meliadus fumed.
What did King Huon expect of him? How could he deal with
these automata?

"Do you not have dances in Asiacommunista?" he said, his
voice trembling with suppressed anger.

"Not of the sort I suppose you prefer," replied Orkai Heong
Phoon, and though there was no inflection in his voice, again
Baron Meliadus was given to think that such activities were
beneath the dignity of the Asiacommunistan nobles. It was
becoming, he thought grimly, exceedingly difficult to remain
polite toward these proud strangers. Meliadus was not used to
suppressing his feelings where mere foreigners were concerned
and he promised himself the pleasure of dealing with these two
in particular should he be given the privilege of leading any
army that conquered the Far East.

Baron Meliadus paused before Adaz Promp who bowed to
the two guests. "May I present one of our mightiest warlords,
the Count Adaz Promp, Grand Constable of the Order of the
Hound, Prince of Parye and Protector of Munchein, Commander of Ten Thousand." The ornate dog-mask inclined
itself again.

"Count Adaz led the force that helped us conquer all the
European mainland in two years when we had allowed for
twenty," Meliadus said. "His hounds are invincible."

"The baron flatters me," said Adaz Promp, "I am sure you
have mightier legions in Asiacommunista, my lords."

"Perhaps, I do not know. Your army sounds as fierce as our
dragon-hounds," Kaow Shalang Gatt said.

"Dragon-hounds? And what are they?" Meliadus enquired,
remembering at last what his king had desired him to do.

"You have none in Granbretan?"

"Perhaps we call them by another name? Could you
describe them?"

Kaow Shalang Gatt made a movement with his staff. "They

are about twice the height of a man – one of our men – with seventy teeth that are like ivory razors. They are very hairy and have claws like a cat's. We use them to hunt those reptiles we have not yet trained for war."

"I see," Meliadus murmured, thinking that such war-beasts would require special tactics to defeat. "And how many such dragon-hounds have you trained for battle?"

"A good number," said his guest.

They moved on, meeting other nobles and their ladies, and each was prepared with a question such as Adaz Promp had asked, to give Meliadus the opportunity of extracting information from the emissaries. But it became plain that although they were willing to indicate that their forces and weaponry were mighty, they were too cautious to provide details as to numbers and capacity. Meliadus realised that it would take more than one evening to gather that sort of information, and he had the feeling that it would be hard to get it at all.

"Your science must be very sophisticated," he said as they moved through the throng. "More advanced than ours, perhaps?"

"Perhaps," said Orkai Heong Phoon, "but I know so little of your science. It would be interesting to compare such things."

"Indeed it would," agreed Meliadus. "I heard, for instance, that your flying machine brought you several thousand miles in a very short space of time."

"It was not a flying machine," said Orkai Heong Phoon.

"No? Then how . . . ?"

"We call it an Earth Chariot – it moves through the ground . . ."

"And how is it propelled? What moves the earth away from it?"

"We are not scientists," put in Kaow Shalang Gatt. "We do not pretend to understand the workings of our machines. We leave such things to the lowlier castes."

Baron Meliadus, feeling slighted again, came to a halt before the beautiful heron mask of the Countess Flana Mikosevaar. He announced her and she curtsied.

"You are very tall," she said in her throaty murmur. "Yes, very tall."

Baron Meliadus attempted to move on, embarrassed by the

countess as he had half-suspected he would be. He had only introduced her to fill the silence following the visitor's last remark. But Flana reached and touched Orkai Heong Phoon's shoulder. "And your shoulders are very very broad," she said. The emissary made no reply, but stood stock still. Had she insulted him? Meliadus wondered. He would have felt some satisfaction if she had. He did not expect the Asiacommunistan to complain, for he realised it was as much in the man's interests to remain on good terms with Granbretan's nobles as it was in Granbretan's interests, at this stage, to remain on good terms with them. "May I entertain you in some way?" asked Flana, gesturing vaguely.

"Thank you, but I can think of nothing at this moment," said the man, and they moved on.

Astonished, Flana watched them continue their progress. She had never been rejected before and she was intrigued. She decided to explore these possibilities further, when she could find a suitable time. They were odd, these taciturn creatures, with their stiff movements. They were like men of metal, she thought. Could anything, she wondered, produce a human emotion in them?

Their great masks of painted leather swayed above the heads of the crowd as Meliadus introduced them to Jerek Nankenseen and his lady, the Duchess Falmoliva Nankenseen who, in her youth, had ridden to battle with her husband.

And when the tour was completed, Baron Meliadus returned to his golden throne wondering, with increased curiosity and sense of frustration, where his rival, Shenegar Trott, had disappeared to, and why King Huon should have deigned not to trust him with the information of Trott's movements. He wanted urgently to rid himself of his charges and hurry to Taragorm's laboratories to discover what progress the Master of the Palace of Time had made and whether there was any possibility of discovering the whereabouts in time or space of the hated Castle Brass.

Chapter Eight
MELIADUS AT THE PALACE OF TIME

EARLY NEXT MORNING, after an unsatisfactory night in which he had given up sleep and failed to find pleasure, Baron Meliadus left to visit Taragorm at the Palace of Time.

In Londra there were few open streets. Houses, palaces, warehouses and barracks were all connected by enclosed passages which, in the richer sections of the city, were of bright colors as if the walls were made of enamelled glass or, in the poorer sections, of oily, dark stone.

Meliadus was borne through these passages in a curtained litter by a dozen girl slaves, all naked and with rouged bodies (the only kind of slaves Meliadus would have to serve him). His intention was to visit Taragorm before those boorish nobles of Asiacommunista were awake. It could be, of course, that they did represent a nation that was helping Hawkmoon and the rest, but he had no proof. If his hopes of Taragorm's discoveries were realised, then he might have proof and thus be able to present it to King Huon, vindicate himself and perhaps, too, rid himself of the troublesome task of playing host to the emissaries.

The passages widened and strange sounds began to be heard – dull booms and regular, mechanical noises. Meliadus knew that he heard Taragorm's clocks.

As he neared the entrance to the Palace of Time, the noise became deafening as a thousand gigantic pendulums swung at a thousand different rates, as machinery whirred and shifted, as jacks struck bells and gongs and cymbals, mechanical birds cried and mechanical voices spoke. It was an incredibly confusing din for, although the palace contained some several thousand clocks of differing sizes, it was itself a gigantic clock, the chief regulator for the rest, and above all the other sounds came the slow, ponderous, echoing clack of the massive escapement lever far above near the roof and the hissing of the monstrous pendulum as it swung through the air in the Hall of the Pendulum where Taragorm conducted most of his experiments.

Meliadus's litter arrived at last before a relatively small set of bronze doors and mechanical men sprang forward to block the way, a mechanical voice cutting through the din of the clocks to demand:

"Who visits Lord Taragorm at the Palace of Time?"

"Baron Meliadus, his brother-in-law, with the permission of the King Emperor," replied the baron, forced to shout.

The doors remained closed for a good deal longer, Meliadus thought, than they should have done, then opened slowly to admit the litter.

Now they passed into a hall with curved walls of metal, like the base of a clock, and the noise increased. The hall was full of *ticks* and *clacks* and *whirrs* and *booms* and *thumps* and *swishes* and *clangs* and, had not the baron's head been encased in its wolf-helm, he would have pressed his hands to his ears. As it was he began to be convinced that shortly he would become deaf.

They passed through this hall into another that was swathed in tapestries (inevitably representing in highly formalised design a hundred different time-keeping devices) which muffled the worst of the noise. Here the girl slaves lowered the litter and Baron Meliadus pushed back the curtains with gauntleted hands and stood there to await the coming of his brother-in-law.

Again (he felt) he had to wait an unconscionable time before the man appeared, stepping sedately through the doors at the far end of the hall, his huge clock mask nodding.

"It is early, brother," said Taragorm. "I regret I kept you waiting, but I had not breakfasted."

Meliadus reflected that Taragorm had never had a decent regard for the niceties of etiquette, then he snapped: "My apologies, brother, but I was anxious to see your work."

"I am flattered. This way, brother."

Taragorm turned and left through the door he had entered, Meliadus close on his heels.

Through more tapestried passages they moved until at last Taragorm pressed his weight against the bar that locked a huge door, the door opened and the air was suddenly full of the sound of a great wind, the noise of a gigantic d.um sounding a painfully slow beat.

Automatically Meliadus looked up and saw the pendulum hurtling through the air above him – its bob fifty tons of brass fashioned in the form of an ornate, blazing sun, creating a draft that fluttered all the tapestries in the halls behind them and raised Meliadus's cloak like a pair of heavy silken wings. The pendulum supplied the wind and the hidden escapement lever, high above, supplied the sound like a drum. Across the vast Hall of the Pendulum was stretched an array of machines in various stages of construction, of benches containing laboratory equipment, of instruments of brass and bronze and silver, of clouds of fine golden wires, of webs of jewelled thread, of time-keeping instruments – water-clocks, pendulum movements, lever movements, ball movements, watches, chronometers, orreries, astrolabes, leaf-clocks, skeleton clocks, table clocks, sun dials – and working on all these were Taragorm's slaves, scientists and engineers captured from a score of nations, many of them the finest of their lands.

Even as Meliadus watched, there would come a flash of purple light from one part of the hall, a shower of green sparks from another, a gout of scarlet smoke from elsewhere. He saw a black machine crumble to dust and its attendant cough, tumble forward into the dust and vanish.

"And what was that?" came a laconic voice from nearby. Meliadus turned to see that Kalan of Vitall, Chief Scientist to the King-Emperor, was also visiting Taragorm.

"An experiment in accelerated time," said Taragorm. "We can create the process, but we cannot control it. Nothing, so far, has worked. See there . . ." he pointed to a large ovoid machine of yellow, glassy substance . . . "that creates the opposite effect and again, unfortunately, cannot be controlled as yet. The man you see beside it," he indicated what Meliadus had taken to be a lifelike statue (some mechanical figure from a clock being repaired), "has been frozen thus for weeks!"

"And what of travelling through time?" Meliadus said.

"Over there," Taragorm replied. "You see the set of silver boxes? Each of those houses an instrument we have created that can hurl an object through time, either back or forth – we are not sure for what distances. Living things, however, suffer

43

much when undergoing the same journey. Few of the slaves or animals we have used have lived, and none have not suffered considerable agonies and deformities."

"If only we had believed Tozer," Kalan said, "perhaps then we might have discovered the secret of travelling through time. We should not have made such a joke of him – but, really, I could not believe that that scribbling buffoon had truly discovered the secret!"

"What's that? What?" Meliadus had heard nothing of Tozer. "Tozer the playwright. I thought him dead! What did he know of time travel?"

"He reappeared, trying to reinstate himself in the King Emperor's graces with a story that he had learned how to journey through time from an old man in the West – a mental trick, he said. We brought him here, laughingly asked him to prove the truth of his words by travelling through time. Whereupon, Baron Meliadus, he vanished!"

"You – you made no effort to hold him . . . ?"

"It was impossible to believe him," Taragorm put in. "Would you have?"

"I would have been more careful in testing him."

"It was in his interest to return, we thought. Besides, brother, we were not clutching at straws."

"What do you mean by that – brother?" retorted Meliadus.

"I mean that we are working in the spirit of pure scientific research, whereas you require immediate results in order to continue your vendetta against Castle Brass."

"I, brother, am a warrior – a man of action. It does not suit me to sit about and play with toys or brood over books." Honor satisfied, Baron Meliadus returned his attention to the subject of Tozer.

"You say the playwright learned the secret from an old man in the West?"

"So he said," replied Kalan. "But I think he was lying. He told us it was a mental trick he had developed, but we did not think him capable of such discipline. Still, the fact remains, he faded and vanished before our eyes."

"Why was I not told of this?" Meliadus moaned in frustration.

"You were still on the mainland when it took place," Taragorm pointed out. "Besides, we did not think it was of

44

interest to a man of action like yourself."

"But his knowledge could have clarified your work," Meliadus said. "You seem so casual about having lost the opportunity."

Taragorm shrugged. "What can we do about it now? We are progressing little by little . . ." somewhere there was a bang, a man screamed and a mauve and orange flash illuminated the room . . . "and we shall soon have tamed time as we are taming space."

"In a thousand years, perhaps!" snorted Meliadus. "The West – an old man in the West? We must locate him. What is his name?"

"Tozer told us only that he was called Mygan – a sorcerer of considerable wisdom. But, as I said, I believe he was lying. After all, what's in the West save desolation? Nothing has lived there but malformed creatures since the Tragic Millenium."

"We must go there," Meliadus said. "We must leave no stone unturned, no chance overlooked . . ."

"Not I – I'll not journey to those bleak mountains on a wild goose chase," said Kalan with a shudder. "I have my work to do here, fitting my new engines into ships, ships that will enable us to conquer the rest of the world as swiftly as we conquered Europe. Besides, I thought you, too, had responsibilities at home, Baron Meliadus – our visitors . . ."

"Damn the visitors. They cost me precious time."

"Soon I shall be able to offer you all the time you require, brother," Taragorm told him. "Give us a little while . . ."

"Bah! I can learn nothing here. Your crumbling boxes and exploding machines make spectacular sights, but they are useless to me. Play your games, brother, play your games. I'll bid you good morning!"

Feeling relieved that he no longer had to be polite to his hated brother-in-law, Meliadus turned and stalked out of the Hall of the Pendulum, through the tapestried corridors and halls, back to his litter.

He flung himself into it, grunted for the girls to bear him away.

As he was borne back to his own palace, Meliadus considered the new information.

At the first opportunity he would rid himself of his charges and journey to the West, to see if he could retrace Tozer's steps

45

and discover the old man who held not only the secret of time, but also the means of his at last exacting his full vengeance upon Castle Brass.

Chapter Nine
INTERLUDE AT CASTLE BRASS

AT CASTLE BRASS, in the courtyard, Count Brass and Oladahn of the Bulgar Mountains, straddled their horned horses and rode out, through the red-roofed town, and away to the fens, as was their habit now every morning.

Count Brass had lost some of his brooding manner and had begun to desire company again since the visit of the Warrior in Jet and Gold.

Elvereza Tozer was held captive in a suite of rooms in one of the towers and had seemed content when Bowgentle had given him supplies of paper, pens and ink and told him to earn his keep with a play, promising him an appreciative, if small audience.

"I wonder how Hawkmoon fares," he said, as they rode together in pleasurable companionship. "I regret that I did not draw the straw that would have enabled me to accompany him."

"I, too," said Oladahn. "D'Averc was lucky. A shame there were only two rings that could be used – Tozer's and the Warrior's. If they return with the rest, then we'll all be able to make war on the Dark Empire . . ."

"It was a dangerous idea, friend Oladahn, to suggest, as the Warrior suggested, they visit Granbretan itself and try to discover Mygan of Llandar in Yel."

"I have heard it said that it is often safer to dwell in the lion's lair than outside it," Oladahn said.

"Safer still to live in a land where there are no lions," Count Brass retorted with a small quirk of his lips.

"Well, I hope the lion does not devour them, that is all, Count

Brass," said Oladahn frowning. "It may be perverse of me, but I still envy him his opportunity."

"I have a feeling that we shall not long have to put up with this inaction," Count Brass said, guiding his horse along the narrow track between the reeds, "for it seems to me that our security is threatened from not one quarter but many . . ."

"It is not a possibility that worries *me* overmuch," said Oladahn, "but I fear for Yisselda, Bowgentle and the ordinary folk of the town, for they have no relish for the sort of activity we enjoy."

The two men rode on to the sea, enjoying the solitude and at the same time yearning for the din and the action of battle.

Count Brass began to wonder if it were not worth smashing the crystal device that was their security, plunging Castle Brass back into the world they had left, and making a fight of it, even though there was no chance of defeating the hordes of the Dark Empire.

Chapter Ten
THE SIGHTS OF LONDRA

THE ORNITHOPTER'S WINGS thrashed at the air as the flying machine hovered over the spires of Londra.

It was a large machine, built to carry four or five people, and its metal bulk gleamed with scrollwork and baroque designs.

Meliadus bent his head over the side and pointed downward. His guests leaned forward also, barely polite. It seemed that their tall, heavy masks would fall from their shoulders if they leaned any further.

"There you see the palace of King Huon where you are staying," Meliadus said, indicating the crazy magnificence of his King Emperor's domicile. It towered above all the other buildings and was set apart from them, in the very center of the city. Unlike most other buildings, it could not be reached by a series of corridors. Its four towers, glowing with a light of deep gold, were even now above their heads, though they sat in the ornithopter, well above the tops of the other buildings. Its tiers were thick with bas-reliefs depicting all manner of dark activities beloved of the Empire. Gigantic and grotesque statues were placed on corners of parapets, seeming about to topple into the courtyards far, far below. The palace was blotched with every imaginable color and all the colors clashed in such a way as to make the eye ache in a matter of seconds.

"The Palace of Time," said Meliadus, indicating the superbly ornamented palace that was also a giant clock.

"My own palace." This was brooding black, faced with silver.

"The river you see is, of course, the River Tayme." The river was thick with traffic. Its blood-red waters bore barges of bronze, ebony and teak ships emblazoned with precious metal and semi-precious jewels, with huge white sails on which designs had been sewn or printed.

"Further to your left," said Baron Meliadus, deeply resenting this silly task, "is our Hanging Tower. You will see that it appears to hang from the sky and is not rooted upon the ground. This was the result of an experiment of one of our sorcerers who managed to raise the tower a few feet but could raise it no further. Then, it appeared, he could not recall it to Earth – so it has remained thus ever since."

He showed them the quays where the great, garnet-burnished battleships of Granbretan dispensed their stolen goods, the Quarter of the Unmasked where lived the scum of the city, the dome of the huge theatre where once Tozer's plays had been performed, the Temple of the Wolf, headquarters of his own order, with a monstrous and grotesque stone wolf head dominating the curve of the roof, and the various other temples with similarly grotesque beast heads carved in stone and weighing many tons.

For a dull day they flew over the city, stopping only to refuel the ornithopter and change pilots, with Meliadus growing hourly impatient. He showed them all the wonders that filled that ancient and unpleasant city, seeking, as his King Emperor had demanded, to impress the visitors with the Dark Empire's might.

As evening came and the setting sun stained the city with unhealthy shades, Baron Meliadus sighed with relief and instructed the pilot to direct the ornithopter to the landing stage on the roof of the palace.

It landed with a great flurry of metal wings, a wheezing and a clattering and the two emissaries climbed stiffly out, like the machine, semblances of natural life.

They walked to the hooded entrance of the palace and moved down the winding ramp until they were at last again in the corridors of shifting light, were met by their guard of honor, six high-ranking warriors of the Order of the Mantis, their insect masks reflecting the brightness from the walls, escorting them back to their own chambers where they would rest and eat.

Leaving them at the door of their apartments, Baron Meliadus bowed and hurried away, having promised that tomorrow they should discuss matters of science, and compare the progress of Asiacommunista with the achievements of Granbretan.

Flinging himself through the hallucinatory passages he almost bowled over the King Emperor's relative, Flana, Countess of Kanbery.

"My lord!"

He paused, made to pass her, stopped. "My lady – my apologies."

"You are in a hurry, my lord!"

"I am, Flana."

"You are in uneven temper, it seems."

"My temper is poor."

"You would console yourself?"

"I have business to attend to . . ."

"Business should be conducted with a cool head, my lord?"

"Perhaps."

"If you would cool your passion . . ."

He started to continue his progress, then stopped again. He had experienced Flana's methods of consolation before. Perhaps she was right. Perhaps he did need her. On the other hand he needed to make preparations for his expedition to the West as soon as the emissaries had departed. Still, they would be here for some days at least. Also, the previous night had proved unsatisfactory and his morale was low. At least he could prove himself a lover.

"Perhaps . . ." he said again, this time more thoughtfully.

"Then let us make haste to my apartments, my lord," said

she with a trace of eagerness.

With mounting interest, Meliadus took her arm.

"Ah, Flana," he murmured. "Ah, Flana."

Chapter Eleven
THOUGHTS OF THE COUNTESS FLANA

FLANA'S MOTIVES in seeking the company of Meliadus had been mixed, for it was not the baron that she was chiefly interested in, but in his charges, the two stiff-limbed giants from the East.

She asked him about them as they lay in their sweat in her enormous bed and he confided his frustrations, his hatred of his task and his hatred of the emissaries, told her of his real ambition, which was to avenge himself of his enemies, the slayers of her husband, the inhabitants of Castle Brass, told her of his discovery that Tozer had found an old man in the West, in the forgotten province of Yel, who might have the secret of reaching his foes.

And he murmured of his fears that he was losing his power, his prestige (though he knew he should not speak such secret thoughts to Flana of all women) and that the King Emperor was these days trusting others, such as Shenegar Trott, with the knowledge that he once only gave to Meliadus.

"Oh, Flana," he said, shortly before he fell into a moody sleep, "if you were Queen, together we could fulfill our Empire's mightiest destiny."

But Flana scarcely heard him, was scarcely thinking, merely lay there and moved her heavy body from time to time, for Meliadus had failed to ease the aching in her soul, had barely eased the craving in her loins and her mind was on the emissaries who lay sleeping only two tiers above her head.

At length she rose from the bed, leaving Meliadus snoring and moaning in his sleep, and dressed herself again in gown and mask, and slipped from her room to glide along the corridors, up the ramps, until she came at last to the doors that were guarded by the Mantis warriors. The insect masks turned questioningly.

"You know who I am," said she.

They did know and they withdrew from the doors. She chose one and pressed it open, entering the exciting darkness of the emissaries' apartments.

Chapter Twelve
A REVELATION

MOONLIGHT ALONE ILLUMINATED the room, falling on a bed in which a figure stirred, showing her the discarded ornaments, armor and mask of the man who lay there.

She moved closer.

"My lord?" she whispered.

Suddenly the figure shot up in the bed and she saw his startled face, saw his hands fly up to cover his features, and she gasped in recognition.

"I know you!"

"Who are you?" He leapt from beneath the silken sheets, naked in the moonlight, ran forward to seize her. "A woman!"

"Aye . . ." purred she. "And you are a man." She laughed softly. "Not a giant at all, though of goodly height. Your mask and armor made you seem more than a foot taller."

"What do you want?"

"I sought to entertain you, sir – and be entertained. But I am disappointed, for I believed you to be some creature other than human. Now I know you to be the man I saw in the Throne Room two years ago – the man Meliadus brought before the King-Emperor."

"So you were there that day." His grip tightened on her and his hand rose to yank off her mask and cover her mouth. She nibbled the fingers. Stroked the muscles of the other arm. The hand on her mouth relaxed.

"Who are you?" he whispered. "Do others know?"

"I am Flana Mikosevaar, Countess of Kanbery. None suspects you, daring German. And I will not call in the guards, if that is what you expect, for I have no interest in politics and no sympathy with Meliadus. Indeed, I am grateful to you, for you rid me of a troublesome spouse."

"You are Mikosevaar's widow?"

"I am. And you I knew immediately by the black jewel in your forehead which you sought to hide when I entered. You are Duke Dorian Hawkmoon von Köln, here in disguise, no doubt, to learn the secrets of your enemies."

"I believe I shall have to kill you, madam."

"I have no intention of betraying you, Duke Dorian. At least, not at once. I came to offer myself for your pleasure, that is all. You have rid me of my mask." She turned her golden eyes upward to regard his handsome face. "Now you may rid me of the rest of my garb . . ."

"Madam," he said hoarsely. "I cannot. I am married."

She laughed. "As am I – I have been married countless times."

There was sweat on his forehead as he returned her gaze and his muscles tensed. "Madam – I – I cannot . . ."

There was a sound and they both turned.

The door separating the apartments opened and there stood a gaunt, good-looking man who coughed a little ostentatiously and then bowed. He, too, was completely naked.

"My friend, madam," said Huillam D'Averc, "is of a somewhat rigid moral disposition. However, if I can assist . . ."

She moved toward him, looking him up and down. "You seem a healthy fellow," she said.

He turned his eyes away. "Ah, madam, it is kind of you to say so. But I am not, not a well man. On the other hand," he reached out and took her shoulder, guiding her into his chamber, "I will do what little I can to please you before this failing heart gives up on me . . ."

The door closed, leaving Hawkmoon trembling.

He sat on the edge of his bed, cursing himself for not having slept in his cumbersome disguise, but the exhausting tour of the day had made him dispense with caution of that kind. When the Warrior in Jet and Gold had put the plan to them, it had seemed unnecessarily dangerous. The logic had been sound enough – they must discover if the old man from Yel had been found before they went off searching for him in Western Granbretan. But now it seemed their chances of getting such information were dashed.

The guards must have seen the countess enter. Even if they killed her or imprisoned her, the guards would suspect something. They were in a city that was, to a man, totally dedicated to their destruction. They had no allies and there was no possible hope of escape once their real identities became known.

Hawkmoon racked his brains for a plan that would at least enable them to flee the city before it became alerted, but all seemed hopeless.

Hawkmoon began to pile on his heavy robes and armor. The only weapon he had was the golden baton which the Warrior had given him to complete the impression of a noble dignitary from Asiacommunista. He hefted it, wishing he had a sword.

Pacing the room, he continued to try to think of a feasible plan of escape, but nothing came.

He was still pacing when morning came and Huillam D'Averc put his head through the door and grinned. "Good morning, Hawkmoon? Have you had no rest, man? I sympathize. Neither have I. The countess is a demanding creature. However I am glad to see you ready for a journey, for we must hurry."

"What do you mean, D'Averc? I have tried all night to conceive a plan, but I can think of nothing . . ."

"I have been questioning Flana of Kanbery and she has told me everything we need to know, for Meliadus, apparently, has confided much in her. She has also agreed to help us escape."

"How?"

"Her private ornithopter. It is ours for the taking."

"Can you trust her?"

"We must. Listen – Meliadus has not yet had time to seek out Mygan of Llandar. By good fortune, it was our arrival that has kept him here. But he knows of him – knows, at least, that Tozer learned his secret from an old man in the West – and means to find him. We have the chance to find Mygan first. We can go part of the way by Flana's ornithopter which I will fly and continue the rest of the journey on foot."

"But we are weaponless – without proper clothes!"

"Weapons and clothes I can obtain from Flana – masks also. She has a thousand trophies of past conquests in her chambers."

"We must go to her chambers now!"

"No. We must wait for her to return here."

"Why?"

"Because, my friend, Meliadus may still be sleeping in her apartments. Have patience. We are in luck. Pray that it will hold!"

Not much later Flana returned, took off her mask and kissed D'Averc almost hesitantly, as a young girl might kiss a lover. Her features seemed softer and her eyes less haunted, as if she had found some quality in D'Averc's lovemaking that she had not experienced before – possibly gentleness, which was not a quality of the men of Granbretan.

"He is gone," she said. "And I have half a mind, Huillam, to keep you here, for myself. For many years I have contained a need which I could not express, never satisfy. You have come close to satisfying it . . ."

He bent and kissed her lightly on the lips and his voice seemed sincere when he said: "And you, too, Flana, have given me something . . ." He straightened stiffly, having donned his heavy, built-up garments, placed his tall mask upon his head. "Come, we must hurry, before the palace wakes."

Hawkmoon followed D'Averc's example, donning his own helmet, and once again the two resembled strange, half-human creatures, the emissaries from Asiacommunista.

Now Flana led them from the apartments, past the Mantis guards, who fell in behind them, and through the twisting, shining corridors until her own apartments were reached. They ordered the guards to remain outside.

"They will report that they followed us here," D'Averc said. "You will be suspected, Flana!"

She doffed her heron mask and smiled. "No," she said and crossed the deep carpet to a polished chest set with diamonds. She raised the lid and took out a long pipe, at the end of which was a soft bulb. "This bulb contains a poison spray," she said. "Once inhaled, the poison turns the victim mad so that he runs wild and berserk before dying. The guards will run through many corridors before they perish. I have used it before. It always works."

She spoke so sweetly of murder that Hawkmoon was forced to shudder.

"All I need do, you see," she continued, "is to push the

hollow rod through the keyhole and squeeze the bulb."

She placed the apparatus on the lid of the chest and led them through several splendid, eccentrically furnished rooms, until they came to a chamber with a huge window that looked out onto a broad balcony. There on the balcony, its wings neatly folded, fashioned to resemble a beautiful scarlet and silver heron, was Flana's ornithopter.

She hurried to another part of the room and drew back a curtain. There, in a great pile, was her booty – clothes, masks and weapons of all her departed lovers and husbands.

"Take what you need," she murmured, "and hurry."

Hawkmoon selected a doublet of blue velvet, hose of black doe-skin, a sword-belt of brocaded leather which held a long, beautifully balanced blade and a poignard. For his mask he took one of his slain enemy's – Asrovaak Mikosevaar's – glowering vulture masks.

D'Averc dressed himself in a suit of deep yellow with a cloak of lustrous blue, boots of deerhide and a blade similar to Hawkmoon's. He, too, took a vulture mask, reasoning that two of the same Order would be likely to be travelling together. Now they looked fully great nobles of Granbretan.

Flana opened the window and they stepped out into the cold, foggy morning.

"Farewell," whispered Flana. "I must get back to the guards. Farewell, Huillam D'Averc. I hope we shall meet again."

"I hope so, also, Flana," replied D'Averc with unusual gentleness of tone. "Farewell."

He climbed into the cockpit of the ornithopter and started the motor. Hawkmoon hastily got in behind him.

The thing's wings began to beat at the air and with a clatter of metal it rose into the gloomy sky of Londra, turning West.

Chapter Thirteen
KING HUON'S DISPLEASURE

MANY EMOTIONS CONFLICTED in Baron Meliadus as he entered the Throne Room of his King Emperor, abased himself and began the long trudge toward the Throne Globe.

The white fluid of the globe surged more agitatedly than usual, alarming the Baron. He was at once furious that the emissaries had disappeared, nervous of his monarch's wrath, anxious to pursue his quest for the old man who could give him the means of reaching Castle Brass. Also he feared lest he lose his power and his pride and (the king had been known to do it before) be banished to the Quarter of the Unmasked. His nervous fingers brushed his wolf-helm and his step faltered as he neared the Throne Globe and looked anxiously up at the foetus-like shape of his monarch.

"Great King Emperor. It is your servant Meliadus."

He fell to his knees and bowed to the ground.

"Servant? You have not served us very well, Meliadus!"

"I am sorry, Noble Majesty, but . . ."

"But?"

"But I could have no knowledge that they planned to leave last night, returning by the means with which they came . . ."

"It should have been your business to sense their plans, Meliadus."

"Sense? *Sense* their plans, Mighty Monarch . . . ?"

"Your instinct is failing you, Meliadus. Once it was exact – you acted according to its dictates. Now your silly plans for vengeance fill your brain and being and make you blind to all else. Meliadus, those emissaries slew six of my best guards. How they killed them, I know not – perhaps a mental spell of some kind – but kill them they did, somehow leaving the palace and returning to whatever machine brought them here. They have discovered much about us – and we, Meliadus, have discovered virtually nothing about them."

"We know a little of their military equipment . . ."

"Do we? Men can lie, you know, Meliadus. Men can lie. We are displeased with you. We charged you to perform a duty and you performed it only partially and without your full attention. You spent time at Taragorm's palace, left the emissaries to their own devices when you should have been entertaining them. You are a fool, Meliadus. A fool!"

"Sire, I – "

"It is your stupid obsession with that handful of outlaws who dwell in Castle Brass. Is it the girl you desire? Is that why you seek them with such single-mindedness?"

"I fear they threaten the Empire, noble sire . . ."

"So does Asiacommunista threaten our Empire, Baron Meliadus – with real swords and real armies and real ships that can travel through the earth. Baron, you must forget your vendetta against Castle Brass or, we warn you, you had best be wary of our displeasure."

"But, sire . . ."

"We have warned you, Baron Meliadus. Put Castle Brass from your mind. Instead, try to learn all you can of the emissaries, discover where their machine met them, how they managed to leave the city. Redeem yourself in our eyes, Baron Meliadus – restore yourself to your old prestige . . ."

"Aye, sire," Baron Meliadus said through gritted teeth, controlling his anger and chagrin.

"The audience is at an end, Meliadus."

"Thank you," said Meliadus, blood pounding in his head, "sire."

He backed away from the Throne Globe.

He turned on his heel and began to pace the long hall.

He reached the jewelled doors, pushed past the guards and strode down the gleaming corridors of shifting light.

On he marched, and on, his pace rapid and his movements stiff, his hand white on the hilt of his sword which it gripped tightly.

He paced until he had reached the great reception hall of the palace where waited the nobles craving audience with the King Emperor, descended the steps that led to the gates that opened on the outer worlds, signed for his girls to come forward with his litter, clambered into it and dumped himself heavily on its cushions, and allowed himself to be borne back to his black and silver palace.

Now he hated his King Emperor. Now he loathed the creature who had humiliated him so, thwarted him so, insulted him so. King Huon was a fool not to realise the potential danger offered by Castle Brass. Such a fool was not fit to reign, not fit to command slaves, let alone Baron Meliadus, Grand Constable of the Order of the Wolf.

Meliadus would not listen to King Huon's stupid orders, would do what he thought best and, if the King Emperor objected, then he would defy him.

A little later, Meliadus left his palace on horseback. He rode at the head of twenty men. Twenty handpicked men whom he could trust to follow him anywhere – even to Yel.

Chapter Fourteen
THE WASTES OF YEL

THE COUNTESS FLANA's ornithopter dropped closer and closer to the ground, its belly brushing the tops of tall pines, its wings narrowly missing becoming entangled with the branches of birches, until at last it landed on the wiry heather beyond the forest.

The day was cold and a sharp wind whistled across the heath, biting through their flimsy costumes.

Shivering, they clambered from the flying machine and looked warily about them. No one was in sight.

D'Averc reached into his jerkin and produced a scrap of thin leather on which a map was scrawled.

He pointed. "We go in that direction. Now we must get the ornithopter into the woods and hide it."

"Why cannot we leave it? The chances of anyone finding it for a day or so are slim," Hawkmoon said.

But D'Averc spoke seriously. "I do not wish any harm to come to Countess Flana, Hawkmoon. If the machine were

58

discovered, it could be ill for her. Come."

And so they tugged and shoved at the metal machine until it was in the pinewood and thickly covered with brush. It had borne them as far as it could until its fuel gave out. They had not expected it to carry them the whole way to Yel.

Now they must continue on foot.

For four days they walked through woods and across heaths, the terrain gradually becoming less and less fertile as they neared the borders of Yel.

Then one day Hawkmoon paused and pointed. "Look, D'Averc – the Mountains of Yel."

And there they were in the distance, their purple peaks in cloud, the plain and the foothills beneath them all tawny yellow rock.

It was a wild, beautiful landscape, such as Hawkmoon had never seen before.

He gasped. "So there are some sights in Granbretan not entirely offensive to the eye, D'Averc."

"Aye, it is pretty," D'Averc agreed. "But daunting also. We have to find Mygan there somewhere. Judging by the map, Llandar is still many miles into those mountains."

"Then let us press on," Hawkmoon said, adjusting his sword belt. "Let us press on. We had a small advantage over Meliadus to begin with, but it is possible that even now he is on his way to Yel in hot quest of Mygan."

D'Averc stood on one leg and ruefully rubbed his foot. "True, but I fear these boots will not last the distance. I picked them from pride, for their prettiness, not for their sturdiness. I am learning my mistake."

Hawkmoon clapped him on the shoulder. "I've heard wild ponies roam these parts. Pray we find a couple we can tame."

But no wild ponies could be found and the yellow ground was hard and rocky and the sky above became full of a livid radiance. Hawkmoon and D'Averc began to realise why the folk of Granbretan were so superstitious of this region, for there did seem to be something unnatural about both land and sky.

At last the mountains were entered.

Seen close to, these were also of a yellowish color, though with streaks of dark red and green, all glassy and grim. Strange-looking beasts skittered away from their path as they clambered on over jagged rocks and peculiar man-like creatures, with hairy bodies topped by completely hairless heads, measuring less than a foot high, regarded them from cover.

"They were once men, those creatures," D'Averc said. "Their ancestors dwelt in these parts. But the Tragic Millenium did its work here well."

"How do you know this?" Hawkmoon asked him.

"I have read my books. It was in Yel, worse than any other part of Granbretan, that the Tragic Millenium's effects were felt. That is why it is so desolate, for men will not come here any longer."

"Save Tozer – and the old man, Mygan of Llandar."

"Aye – if Tozer spoke the truth. We could still be on a wild goose chase, Hawkmoon."

"But Meliadus had the same story."

"Perhaps Tozer is merely a consistent liar?"

It was close to nightfall that the mountain creatures came scuttling from their caves high above and attacked Hawkmoon and D'Averc.

They were covered in oily fur, with the beaks of birds and the claws of cats, huge eyes blazing, beaks parting to reveal teeth, emitting a horrible hissing sound. There were three females and about six males as far as they could see in the semi-darkness.

Hawkmoon drew his sword, adjusting his vulture mask as he would adjust an ordinary helm, set his back to a wall of rock.

D'Averc took up a position beside him and then the beasts were on them.

Hawkmoon slashed at the first, carving a long, bloody scar across its chest. It recoiled with a shriek.

A second was taken by D'Averc, stabbed through the heart. Hawkmoon neatly slit the throat of a third, but a fourth's claws were gripping his left arm. He struggled, muscles straining as he tried to turn the dagger he gripped upward to stab the creature's wrist, while meanwhile he slashed at another trying to take him from the other side.

Hawkmoon coughed and felt nauseous, for the beasts stank horribly. He at last wrenched his hand round and dug the point of his dagger into its forearm. It grunted and let go.

Instantly Hawkmoon drove the blade of the dagger deep into one staring eye and left the weapon there as he turned to deal with the other creature.

It was dark now and hard to make out how many of the beasts were left. D'Averc was holding his own shouting filthy insults at the creatures as his blade moved rapidly this way and that.

Hawkmoon's foot slipped on blood and he staggered, catching the small of his back on a spur of rock. With a hiss another beaked beast was on him, clutching him in a bearlike grip, pinning both arms to his sides, the beak snapping at his face and closing with a snap on the vulture visor.

Hawkmoon sweated to break the grip, tore his head from the mask, leaving it in the creature's beak, wrenched the thing's arms apart and punched it heavily in the chest. It staggered back in surprise, not realising that the vulture mask had not been part of Hawkmoon's body.

Quickly Hawkmoon drove his sword into its heart and turned to assist D'Averc, who had two of the things on him.

Hawkmoon lopped one's head completely from its shoulders and was about to attack the next when it released D'Averc and screamed, rushing off into the night, clutching part of his jerkin.

They had accounted for all but one of their disgusting attackers.

D'Averc was panting, wounded slightly in the chest where the claws had ripped his jerkin away. Hawkmoon ripped up a piece of his cloak and padded the wound.

"No great harm done," said D'Averc. He yanked off his battered vulture mask and flung it away. "Those came in useful, but I'll wear mine no longer since I see you've discarded yours. That jewel in your forehead is unmistakeable, so there's no point in my continuing to disguise myself!" He grinned. "I told you the Tragic Millenium had produced some ugly creatures, friend Hawkmoon."

"I believe you," smiled Hawkmoon. "Come, we had best find a place to camp for the night. Tozer marked a safe resting spot on his map. Bring it out into the starlight so we can read it."

D'Averc reached into his jerkin and then his jaw dropped in horror. "Oh, Hawkmoon! We are not so lucky!"

"Why so, my friend?"

"That section of my jerkin the creature carried off contained the pocket in which I had the map supplied by Tozer. We are lost, Hawkmoon!"

Hawkmoon cursed, sheathed his sword and frowned.

"There's nothing for it," he said. "We must trail the beast. It was slightly wounded and might have left a trail of blood. Perhaps it has dropped the map on its way back to its lair. Failing that we shall have to follow it all the way to where it lives and find a means of getting back our map when we arrive!"

D'Averc frowned. "Is it worth it? Can we not remember where we are bound?"

"Not well enough. Come, D'Averc."

Hawkmoon began to clamber over the sharp rocks in the direction in which the creature had disappeared and D'Averc came reluctantly after him.

Luckily the sky was clear and the moon bright and Hawkmoon at last saw some gleaming patches on the rocks that must have been blood. A bit further on he saw more patches.

"This way, D'Averc," he called.

His friend sighed, shrugged and followed.

The search went on until dawn, when Hawkmoon lost the trail and shook his head. They were high up on a mountain slope, with a good view of two valleys below them. He ran his hand through his blond hair and he sighed.

"No sign of the thing. And yet I was sure . . ."

"Now we are worse off," D'Averc said absently, rubbing his weary eyes. "No map – and no longer, even, on our original trail . . ."

"I am sorry, D'Averc. I thought it the best plan." Hawkmoon's shoulders sagged. Then suddenly he brightened and pointed.

"There! I saw something moving. Come on." And he was sprinting along the shelf of rock to disappear from D'Averc's sight.

D'Averc heard a shout of surprise and then a sudden silence.

The Frenchman drew his sword and followed after his friend, wondering what he had met with.

Then he saw the source of Hawkmoon's amazement. There, far below in a valley, was a city all made of metal, with shiny surfaces of red, gold, orange, blue and green, with curving metal roadways and sharp metal towers. It was plain to see, even from here, that the city was deserted and falling to pieces, with rusting walls and adornments.

Hawkmoon stood looking down at it. He pointed. There was

their antagonist of the night before, sliding down the rocky sides of the mountain toward the city.

"That must be where he lives," Hawkmoon said.

"I like not to follow him down there," D'Averc murmured. "There could be poison air – the air that makes your flesh crumple from your face, that causes vomiting and death . . ."

"The poison air does not exist any more, D'Averc, and you know it. It only lasts for a while and then disappears. Surely there has been no poison air here for centuries." He began to clamber down the mountain in pursuit of his foe who still clutched the piece of jerkin containing Tozer's map.

"Oh, very well," groaned D'Averc. "Let's seek death together!" And once again he began to follow in his friend's wake. "You are a wild, impatient gentleman, Duke von Köln!"

While loose stones rattled down and made the creature they pursued run all the faster towards the city, Hawkmoon and D'Averc gave chase as best they could, for they were unused to mountainous terrain and D'Averc's boots were almost in shreds.

They saw the beast enter the shadows of the metal city and disappear.

A few moments later they, too, had reached the city and looked up, in some trepidation, at the huge metal structures that loomed into the sky, creating menacing shadows below.

Hawkmoon noticed some more bloodstains and threaded his way between the struts and pylons of the city, peering with difficulty in the murky light.

And then suddenly there was a clicking sound, a hissing sound, a peculiar kind of subdued growl –

– and the creature was upon him, its claws about his throat, digging deeper and deeper. He felt one pierce, then another. He whipped up his own hands and tried to prise the clawed fingers away, felt the beak snap at the back of his neck.

Then there was a wild shriek and a yell and the claws released his throat.

Hawkmoon staggered round to see D'Averc, sword in hand, looking down at the body of the beaked beast.

"The disgusting creature had no brains," said D'Averc lightly. "What a fool it was to attack you and leave me free to slay it from behind." He extended his arm and delicately skewered the missing piece of cloth that had fallen from the dead thing's claw. "Here's our map, as good as ever!"

Hawkmoon wiped blood from his throat. The claws had not pierced too deeply. "The poor thing," he said.

"No softness now, Hawkmoon! You know how it alarms me to hear you speaking thus. Remember the creatures attacked us."

"I wonder why. There should be no shortage of their natural prey in these mountains – there are all kinds of edible creatures. Why feast on us?"

"Either we were the nearest meat they saw," D'Averc suggested, looking about him at the lattice of metal everywhere, "or else they have learned to hate men."

D'Averc re-sheathed his sword with a flourish and began to make his way through the forest of metal struts that supported the towers and streets of the city above them. Refuse lay everywhere and there were bits of dead animals' offal, rotting, unidentifiable stuff.

"Let's explore this city while we're here," D'Averc said, climbing up one girder. "We could sleep here."

Hawkmoon consulted the map. "It's marked," he said. "Halapandur's its name. Not too far to the east of where our mysterious philosopher has his cavern."

"How far?"

"About a day's march in these mountains."

"Then let's rest here and press on tomorrow," D'Averc suggested.

Hawkmoon frowned for a moment. Then he shrugged. "Very well." He, too, began to clamber up through the girders until they reached one of the strange, curving metal streets.

"We'll strike out for yonder tower," suggested D'Averc.

They began to walk along the gently sloping ramp towards a tower that gleamed turquoise and sultry scarlet in the sunshine.

Chapter Fifteen
THE DESERTED CAVERN

AT THE BASE of the tower was a small door that had been driven inwards as if by the punching of a giant fist. Clambering through the aperture, Hawkmoon and D'Averc tried to peer through the gloom to see what the tower contained.

"There," said Hawkmoon. "A stairway – or something very like one."

They stumbled over rubble and discovered that it was not a stairway leading up into the higher parts of the tower, but a ramp, not unlike the ramps that connected one building to another in the city itself.

"From what I've read this place was built only shortly before the Tragic Millenium," D'Averc told Hawkmoon as they continued up the ramp. "It was a city wholly given over to scientists – a Research City, I believe they called it. Every kind of scientist came here from all parts of the world. The idea was that new discoveries would be made by cross-fertilisation. If my memory serves me, the legends say that many strange inventions were made here, though most of their secrets are now completely lost."

Up they went until the ramp led them onto a wide platform which was completely surrounded by windows of glass. Most of the windows were cracked or completely blown out, but from this platform it was possible to see the whole of the rest of the city.

"Almost certainly this was used to view the goings on all over Halapandur," Hawkmoon said. He looked about him. Everywhere were the remains of instruments whose function he could not recognize. They bore the stamp of things prehistoric, all of dull, plain cases with austere characters engraved on them, totally unlike the baroque decoration and flowing numerals and letters of modern times. "Some sort of room controlling the functions of the rest of Halapandur."

D'Averc pursed his lips and pointed. "Ay – you can see its uses. Look, Hawkmoon."

Some distance away, on the opposite side of the city from the one they had entered, could be seen a line of horsemen in the helmets and armor of Dark Empire troops.

It was obvious what they were, but they could make out no details from this height.

"My guess is that Meliadus leads them," Hawkmoon said, fingering his sword. "He cannot know exactly where Mygan is, but he can have discovered that Tozer was in this city at some time, and he'll have trackers with him who'll soon discover Mygan's cave. We cannot afford to rest here now, D'Averc. We must press on at once."

D'Averc nodded. "A shame." He stooped and picked up a small object he had seen on the floor, placing it in his tattered jerkin. "I think I recognise this."

"What is it?"

"It could be one of the charges used for the old guns they used," D'Averc said. "If so, it will be useful."

"But you have no old gun!"

"One does not always need one!" said D'Averc mysteriously.

They ran back down the ramp to the entrance of the tower. Risking being seen by the Dark Empire warriors, they dashed along the large, outer ramps as fast as they could, then swung back again down the girders and out of sight.

"I don't think we were seen," D'Averc said. "Come on – we go this way for Mygan's lair."

They began to race up the side of the mountain, slithering and sliding in their anxiety to reach the old sorcerer before Meliadus.

Night came, but they moved on.

They were starving, for they had eaten practically nothing since they had set out for Llandar Valley, and they were beginning to weaken.

But they struggled on and just before dawn came to the valley marked on the map. The valley where the sorcerer Mygan was said to live.

Hawkmoon began to smile. "Those Dark Empire riders will have camped for the night, almost certainly. We'll have time to see Mygan, get his crystals, and be away before they ever arrive!"

"Let's hope so," said D'Averc, thinking privately that Hawkmoon needed rest, for his eyes were a little feverish. But he followed him down to the valley and consulted the map. "Up there," he said. "That's where Mygan's cave's supposed to be, but I see nothing."

"The map has it halfway up yonder cliff," said Hawkmoon. "Let us climb up and see."

They crossed the floor of the valley, leaping over a small, clear stream that ran down a fissure in the rock the length of the valley. Here there were, indeed, signs of Man, for there was a path down to the river and a wooden apparatus that had evidently been used for drawing up water from the stream.

They followed the path up to the side of the cliff. Now they found old, worn handholds in the rock. They had not been carved recently, but had been there, it appeared, for ages, well before Mygan had been born.

They began to climb.

The going was difficult, but at last they reached a ledge of rock on which a huge boulder stood, and there, behind the boulder, was the dark entrance to a cavern!

Hawkmoon went forward, eager to enter, but D'Averc put a cautionary hand on his shoulder. "Best take care," he said and drew his sword.

"An old man cannot harm us," Hawkmoon said.

"You are tired, my friend, and exhausted, otherwise you would realise that an old man of the wisdom Tozer claimed for him will possibly have weapons which could harm us. He has no liking for men, from what Tozer said, and there is not reason why he should think us anything more than enemies."

Hawkmoon nodded, drew his own blade, and then advanced.

The cavern was dark and seemingly empty, but then they saw a glimmer of light from the back. Approaching the source of this light, they discovered a sharp bend in the cavern.

Rounding the bend they saw that the first cavern led on to a second, much larger. This was fitted up with all sorts of things, instruments of the kind they had seen in Halapandur, a couple of cots, cooking materials, chemical equipment and much more. The source of the light was a globe in the center of the cave.

"Mygan!" called D'Averc, but there was no reply.

They searched the cave, wondering if there was yet another extension, but found nothing.

"He has gone!" Hawkmoon said in desperation, his nervous fingers rubbing at the black jewel in his forehead. "Gone, D'Averc, and who knows where. Perhaps after Tozer left him, he decided that it was no longer safe to remain and has moved on."

"I think not," D'Averc said. "He would have taken some of this stuff with him, would he not?" He looked around the cave. "And that cot looks recently slept in. There is no dust anywhere. Mygan has probably gone off on some local expedition and will be back soon. We must wait for him."

"And what of Meliadus – if that was Meliadus we saw?"

"We must simply hope he moves slowly on the trail and takes some time to discover this cave!"

"If he's as eager as you said Flana told you, then he'll not be far behind us," Hawkmoon pointed out. He went to a bench on which there were various dishes of meat, vegetables and herbs, helping himself greedily. D'Averc followed his example.

"We'll rest here and wait," D'Averc said. "It is all we can do now my friend."

A day passed, and a night, and Hawkmoon hourly grew impatient as the old man did not return.

"Suppose he has been captured," he suggested to D'Averc. "Suppose Meliadus found him wandering in the mountains."

"If so, then Meliadus is bound to bring him back here and we shall win the old man's gratitude by rescuing him from the baron." D'Averc replied with forced cheerfulness.

"There were twenty men we saw, armed with flame-lances if I was not mistaken. We cannot take twenty, D'Averc."

"You are in low spirits, Hawkmoon. We have taken twenty before – more!"

"Aye," Hawkmoon agreed, but it was plain that the journey had taken much out of him. Perhaps, too, the deception at the Court of King Huon had been a greater strain on him than on D'Averc, for D'Averc appeared to relish deception of that kind.

At length, Hawkmoon strode to the outer cave and onto the ledge beyond. Some instinct seemed to draw him out, for he looked down into the valley and saw them.

Now it was close enough to be sure.

The leader of the men was, indeed, Baron Meliadus. His ornate wolf mask glinted ferociously as it turned up and saw Hawkmoon at the instant Hawkmoon looked down.

The great, roaring voice echoed through the mountains. It was a voice full of mingled rage and triumph, the voice of a wolf that has scented its prey.

"Hawkmoon!" came the cry. "Hawkmoon!"

Meliadus flung himself from his saddle and began to scale the cliff. "Hawkmoon!"

Behind him came his well-armed men and Hawkmoon knew there was little chance of fighting them all off. He called back into the cavern. "D'Averc – Meliadus is here. Quickly man, he'll trap us in these caves. We must reach the top of the cliff."

D'Averc came running from the cavern, buckling on his sword belt, glanced down, thought for a moment, then nodded. Hawkmoon ran to the face of the cliff, seeking handholds on the rough surface, hauling himself upward.

A flame-lance beam splashed against the rock close to his hand, singeing the hairs on his wrist. Another landed beneath him, but he climbed on.

Perhaps at the top of the cliff he could stand and make a fight, but he needed to protect his life and D'Averc's for as long as possible, for the security of Castle Brass could depend on it.

"Haaawkmoooon!" came the echoing cry of the vengeful Meliadus. "Haaaawkmooooooon!"

Hawkmoon climbed on, scraping his hands on the rock, gashing his leg, but not pausing, taking incredible risks as he clambered up the cliff face, D'Averc close behind him.

At last they reached the top and saw a plateau stretching away from them. If they attempted to cross it, the flame-lances were bound to cut them down.

"Now," Hawkmoon said grimly, drawing his sword, "we stand and fight."

D'Averc grinned. "At last. I thought you were losing your nerve, my friend."

They glanced over the edge of the cliff and saw that Baron Meliadus had reached the ledge by Mygan's cavern and was darting in, sending his men on ahead in pursuit of his two hated foes. Doubtless he hoped to find some of the others there – Oladahn, Count Brass – or even, perhaps Yisselda, whom Hawkmoon knew was loved by the baron, however much he refused to admit it.

Soon the first of the wolf warriors had reached the cliff and Hawkmoon delivered a jarring kick to his helmet. He did not fall, however, but reached out and clutched Hawkmoon's foot, doubtless trying to drag himself back to safety or drag Hawkmoon with him over the cliff.

D'Averc sprang forward stabbing the man in the shoulder. He grunted, released the grip on Hawkmoon, sought to grasp a spur of rock on the cliff edge, missed and tumbled backwards, arms flailing, to yell one long yell all the way to the floor of the valley, far, far below.

But now others were clambering over the edge. D'Averc engaged one, while Hawkmoon suddenly found himself with two to contend with.

Back and forth along the edge of the cliff they fought, the valley hundreds of feet below them.

Hawkmoon took one in the throat, between helm and gorget, neatly skewered another through the belly, where his armor did not reach, but two more quickly took their place.

They fought for an hour thus, keeping back as many as they could from gaining the top of the cliff, engaging with their swords those they could not dissuade from getting to the top.

Then they were surrounded, the swords pressing in on them like the teeth of some gigantic shark, until their throats were threatened by a band of blades and Meliadus's voice came from somewhere, full of gloating malice. "Surrender, gentlemen, or you'll be butchered, I promise."

Hawkmoon and D'Averc lowered their swords, glancing hopelessly at each other.

They both knew that Meliadus hated them with a terrible, consuming hatred. Now that they were his prisoners in his own land, there was no possibility of escape.

Meliadus seemed to realize this, too, for he cocked his wolf mask on one side and chuckled.

"I do not know how you came to Granbretan, Hawkmoon and D'Averc, but I do know you now for a pair of fools! Were you too seeking the old man? Why, I wonder? You already have what he has."

"Perhaps he has other things," said Hawkmoon, deliberately attempting to obscure the matter as much as possible, for the less Meliadus knew, the more chance they had of deceiving him.

"Other things? You mean he has other devices useful to the Empire? Thanks for telling me, Hawkmoon. The old man himself will doubtless be more specific."

"The old man has left, Meliadus," said D'Averc smoothly. "We warned him you might be coming."

"Left, eh? I'm not sure of that. But if that's the case, you'll know where he has gone, Sir Huillam."

"Not I," said D'Averc, looking peeved as the warriors bound him and Hawkmoon together and tied a noose under their arms.

"We'll see." Meliadus chuckled again. "I appreciate the excuse you offer me to begin a little torture on you here and now. A soupçon of vengeance for the moment. Later, we'll explore the full possibilities when we return to my palace. Then, too, perhaps I'll have the old man and his secret of travelling through the dimensions . . ." Privately he told himself that he was bound, in this way, to reinstate himself with the King Emperor and achieve Huon's forgiveness for leaving the city without permission.

His gauntleted hand reached out to stroke Hawkmoon's face almost lovingly. "Ah, Hawkmoon – soon you shall feel my punishment; *soon* . . ."

Hawkmoon shuddered to the roots of his being, then spat full into the grinning wolf mask.

Meliadus recoiled, hand going up to mask, then sweeping out and striking Hawkmoon across the mouth. He growled in rage. "Another moment of pain for that, Hawkmoon. And those moments, I promise you, will seem to last for aeons!"

Hawkmoon turned his head away in disgust and pain, was thrust roughly forward by the guards and pushed, together with Sir Huillam D'Averc, over the edge of the cliff.

The rope around their bodies stopped them from falling far, but they were lowered un-gently to the ledge and Meliadus joined them shortly.

"I must still find the old man," said the baron. "I suspect he's lurking somewhere hereabouts. We'll leave you well bound in the cavern, put a couple of guards at the entrance just in case you somehow free yourselves from your bonds, and set off to look for him. There is no escape for you now, Hawkmoon, none for you either, D'Averc. You are both mine at last! Drag them inside. Bind them with all the rope you can find. Remember –

guard them well, for they are Meliadus's playthings!"

He watched as they were trussed and dragged into the nearer cavern. Meliadus placed three men at the entrance of the cavern and began to clamber back down the cliff in high spirits.

It would not be much longer, he promised himself, before all his enemies were in his power, all their secrets had been tortured from them, and then the King Emperor would know that he had spoken the truth.

And if the King Emperor did not think well of him – what matter?

Meliadus had plans to right that error, also.

Chapter Sixteen
MYGAN OF LLANDAR

NIGHT FELL OUTSIDE the cavern and Hawkmoon and D'Averc lay in the shadow cast by the light from the second cave.

The broad backs of the guards filled the entrance and the ropes of their bonds were tight-bound and considerable.

Hawkmoon tried to struggle, but his movements were virtually restricted to moving his mouth, his eyes and his neck a little. D'Averc was in a similar position.

"Well, my friend, we were not cautious enough," D'Averc said with as light a tone as he could muster.

"No," Hawkmoon agreed. "Starvation and weariness makes fools of even the wisest of men. We have only ourselves to blame . ."

"We deserve our suffering," D'Averc said, somewhat doubtfully. "But do our friends? We must think of escape, Hawkmoon, no matter how hopeless it seems."

Hawkmoon sighed. "Aye. If Meliadus should succeed in reaching Castle Brass . . ."

He shuddered.

It seemed to him from his brief encounter with the Gran-

72

bretanian nobleman, that Meliadus was even more deranged than previously. Was it his defeat, several times, by Hawkmoon and the folk of Castle Brass? Was it the thwarting of his victory when Castle Brass had been spirited away? Hawkmoon could not guess. He only knew that his old enemy seemed less in control of his mind than earlier. There was no telling what he would do in such an unbalanced condition.

Hawkmoon turned his head, frowning, thinking he had heard a noise from within the far cavern. From where he lay, he could see a little of the lighted cave.

He craned his neck, hearing the sound again. D'Averc murmured, very softly so that the guards should not hear, "There is someone in there, I'll swear . . ."

And then a shadow fell across them and they stared up into the face of a tall, old man with a great, rugged face that seemed carved from stone and a mane of white hair that helped his leonine appearance.

The old man frowned, looking the bound men up and down. He pursed his lips and looked out to where the three guards stood at attention, looked back at Hawkmoon and D'Averc. He said nothing, simply folded his arms across his chest. Hawkmoon saw that there were crystal rings on his fingers – all but the little finger of the left hand bore rings, even the thumbs. This must be Mygan of Llandar! But how had he got into the cave? A secret entrance?

Hawkmoon looked at him desperately, mouthing his pleas for help.

The giant smiled again and bent forward a little so that he could hear Hawkmoon's whisper.

"Please, sir, if you be Mygan of Llandar, know that we are friends to you – prisoners of your enemies."

"And how do I know you speak truth?" said Mygan, also in a whisper.

One of the guards stirred outside, beginning to turn, doubtless sensing something. Mygan withdrew into the cavern. The guard grunted.

"What are you two muttering about? Discussing what the baron will do with ye, eh? Well, you can't imagine what entertainments he's got fixed up for you, Hawkmoon."

Hawkmoon made no reply.

When the guard had turned back, chuckling, Mygan bent

73

closer again.

"You're Hawkmoon?"

"You've heard of me?"

"Something. If you're Hawkmoon, you may be speaking the truth, for though I be of Granbretan, I hold no brief for the Lords who rule in Londra. But how do you know who my enemies are?"

"Baron Meliadus of Kroiden has learned of the secret you imparted to Tozer who was your guest here not long ago . . ."

"Imparted! He wheedled it from me, stole one of my rings when I slept, used it to escape. Wanted to ingratiate himself with his masters in Londra, I gather . . ."

"You are right. Tozer told them of a power, boasted that it was a mental attribute, demonstrated his power and turned up in the Kamarg . . ."

"Doubtless by accident. He had no conception of how to use the ring properly."

"So we gathered."

"I believe you, Hawkmoon, and I fear this Meliadus."

"You'll free us so that we can attempt to escape from here, protect you against him?"

"I doubt if I need your protection."

Mygan disappeared from Hawkmoon's view.

"What does he plan, I wonder," said D'Averc, who had deliberately remained silent until now.

Hawkmoon shook his head.

Mygan reappeared, a long knife in his hand. He stretched out and began slicing through Hawkmoon's bonds until at last the Duke von Köln was able to free himself, keeping a wary eye on the guards outside.

"Hand me the knife," he whispered, and took it from Mygan's hand, began cutting away D'Averc's ropes.

From outside they heard voices.

"Baron Meliadus is returning," one of the guards said. "He sounds in an evil temper."

Hawkmoon darted an anxious glance at D'Averc and they sprang up.

Alerted by the movement, one of the guards turned, crying out in surprise.

The two men darted forward. Hawkmoon's hand stopped the guard from drawing his sword. D'Averc's arm went round another's throat and drew his sword for him. The sword rose and fell even before the guard could scream.

While Hawkmoon wrestled with the first guard, D'Averc engaged the third. The clang of swords began to sound in the air and they heard Meliadus's shout of surprise.

Hawkmoon threw his opponent to the ground and placed a knee in his groin, drew the dagger that was still sheathed at his side, pried back the mask and struck the man in the throat.

Meanwhile, D'Averc had despatched his man, stood panting over the corpse.

Mygan called from the back of the cavern. "I see you wear crystal rings, like those I have. Do you know how to control them?"

"We know only how to return to the Kamarg! A turn to the left . . ."

"Aye. Well, Hawkmoon, I would help you. You must turn the crystals first to the right and then to the left. Repeat the movement six times and then . . ."

The great bulk of Meliadus loomed in the entrance to the cavern.

"Oh, Hawkmoon – you plague me still. The old man! Seize him, men!"

The rest of Meliadus's warriors began to surge into the cavern. D'Averc and Hawkmoon fell back before them, desperately fighting.

The old man shouted in fury: "Trespassers. Back!" He rushed forward with his long knife raised.

"No!" cried Hawkmoon. "Mygan – let us do the blade work. Keep away. You are defenceless against such as these!"

But Mygan did not retreat. Hawkmoon tried to reach him, saw him go down before a blow from a wolf sword, struck out at the one who had struck Mygan.

The cavern was in confusion as they retreated back into the inner cave. The sound of the swords echoed, counterpointed by Meliadus's enraged shouts.

Hawkmoon dragged the wounded Mygan back to the second cave, warding off the blows that fell upon them both.

Now Hawkmoon faced the singing blade of Meliadus himself, who swung his sword two-handed.

Hawkmoon felt a numbing shock in his left shoulder, felt blood begin to soak his sleeve. He parried a further blow, then struck back, taking Meliadus in the arm.

The baron groaned and staggered back.

"Now, D'Averc!" called Hawkmoon. "Now, Mygan! Turn the crystals! It is our only hope of escape!"

He turned the crystal in his ring first to the right and then to the left, then six times more to right and left. Meliadus growled and came at him again. Hawkmoon raised his sword to block the blow.

And then Meliadus had vanished.

So had the cavern, so had his friends.

He stood alone upon a plain that stretched flat in all directions. It was noon, for a huge sun hung in the sky. The plain was of turf of a kind that grew close to the ground and the smell it gave off reminded Hawkmoon of spring.

Where was he? Had Mygan tricked him? Where were the others?

Then there began to materialize close by the figure of Mygan of Llandar, lying on the turf and clutching at his worst wound. He was covered in a dozen sword cuts, his leonine face pale and twisted with pain. Hawkmoon sheathed his sword and sprang towards him. "Mygan . . ."

"Ah, I'm dying, I fear, Hawkmoon. But at least I've served in the shaping of your destiny. The Runestaff . . ."

"My destiny? What do you mean? And what of the Runestaff? I've heard so much of that mysterious artifact, and yet no one will tell me exactly how it concerns me . . ."

"You'll learn when it's time. Meanwhile . . ."

Suddenly D'Averc appeared, staring around him in astonishment. "The things work! Thank the Runestaff for that. I'd thought us all surely slain."

"You – you must seek . . ." Mygan began to cough. Blood spurted from between his teeth, falling down his chin.

Hawkmoon cradled his head in his arms. "Do not try to speak, Mygan. You are badly wounded. We must find help. Perhaps if we returned to Castle Brass . . ."

Mygan shook his head. "You cannot."

"Cannot return? But why? The rings worked to bring us here. A turn to the left . . ."

"No. Once you have shifted in this way, the rings must be re-set."

"How shall we set them?"

76

"I will not tell you!"

"Will not? You mean cannot?"

"No. It was my intention to bring you through space to this land where you must fulfill part of your destiny. You must seek – ah, ah! The pain!"

"You have tricked us, old man," said D'Averc. "You wish us to play some part in a scheme of your own. But you are dying. We cannot help you now. Tell us how to return to Castle Brass and we shall get someone to doctor you."

"It was no selfish whim that instructed me to bring you here. It was knowledge of history. I have travelled to many places, visited many eras, by means of the rings. I know much. I know what you serve, Hawkmoon, and I know that the time has come for you to venture here."

"Where?" Hawkmoon said desperately. "In what time have you deposited us? What is the land called? It seems to consist entirely of this flat plain!"

But Mygan was coughing blood again and it was plain that death was close.

"Take my rings," he said, breathing with difficulty. "They could be useful. But seek first Narleen and the Sword of the Dawn – that lies to your south. Then turn north, when that's done, and seek the city of Dnark – and the Runestaff." He coughed again, then his body shook with a great spasm and life fled him.

Hawkmoon looked up at D'Averc.

"The Runestaff? Are we then in Asiacommunista where the thing is supposed to dwell?"

"It would be ironic, considering our earlier ruse," said D'Averc, dabbing with his kerchief at a wound on his leg. "Perhaps that is where we are. I care not. We are away from that boorish Meliadus and his bloodthirsty pack. The sun above is warm. Save for our wounds, we are considerably better off than we might have been."

Looking about him, Hawkmoon sighed. "I am no' sure. If Taragorm's experiments are successful, he could find a way through to our Kamarg. I would rather be there than here." He fingered his ring. "I wonder . . ."

D'Averc put out his hand. "No, Hawkmoon. Do not tamper with it. I'm inclined to believe the old man. Besides, he seemed well-disposed toward you. He must have meant you well.

Probably he intended to tell you where this was, give you more explicit directions as to how to reach the places – presuming they were places – he spoke of. If we try to work the rings now, there's no telling where we'll find ourselves – possibly even back in that unpleasant company we left in Mygan's cave!"

Hawkmoon nodded. "Perhaps you're wise, D'Averc. But what do we do now?"

"First we do as Mygan said, and remove his rings. Then we head south – to that place – what did he call it?"

"Narleen. It could be a person. A thing."

"South, at any rate, we go, to find out if this Narleen be place, person or thing. Come." He bent beside the corpse of Mygan of Llandar and began to strip the crystal rings from his fingers. "From what I saw of his cavern, it's almost certain that he found these in the city of Halapandur. That equipment he had in his cave evidently came from there. These must have been one of the inventions of those people before the onset of the Tragic Millenium . . ."

But Hawkmoon was barely listening to him. Instead he was pointing out across the plain.

"Look!"

The wind was blowing up.

In the distance something gigantic and reddish purple came rolling, emitting lightnings.

BOOK TWO

As Dorian Hawkmoon served the Runestaff, so had Mygan of Llandar (though knowingly) and the philosopher of Yel had seen fit to deposit Hawkmoon in a strange, unfriendly land, giving him little information, in order, as he saw it, to further the Runestaff's cause. So many destinies were inter-linked now - the Kamarg's with Granbretan's, Granbretan's with Asiacommunista, Asiacommunistas's with Amarehk - Hawkmoon's with D'Averc's, D'Averc's with Flana's, Flana's with Meliadus's, Meliadus's with King Huon's, King Huon's with Shenegar Trott's, Shenegar Trott's with Hawkmoon's - so many destinies weaving together to do the Runestaff's work which was begun when Meliadus swore upon the Runestaff his great oath of vengeance against the inhabitants of Castle Brass and thus set the pattern of events. Paradoxes and ironies were all apparent in the fabric, would become increasingly clearer to those whose fates were woven into it. And while Hawkmoon wondered where he was placed in time or space, King Huon's scientists perfected more powerful war machines that helped the armies of the Dark Empire spread faster and further across the globe, to stain the map with blood . . .

— *The High History of the Runestaff*

Chapter One
ZHENAK-TENG

HAWKMOON AND D'AVERC watched the strange sphere approach and then wearily drew their swords.

They were in rags, their bodies all bloody, their faces pale with the strain of the fight, and there was little hope in their eyes.

"Ah, I could do with the amulet's power now," said Hawkmoon of the Red Amulet which, on the Warrior's advice, he had left behind at Castle Brass.

D'Averc smiled wanly. "I could do with some ordinary mortal energy," he said. "Still, we must do our best, Duke Dorian." He straightened his shoulders.

The thundering sphere came closer, bouncing over the turf. It was a huge thing, full of flashing colors and there was no question of swords being useful against it.

It rolled to a halt with a dying, growling noise and stopped close by, towering over them.

Then it began to hum and a split appeared at its center, widening out until it seemed the sphere would split in two. From it now appeared white, delicate smoke that drifted in a cloud to the ground.

The cloud now began to disperse and a tall, well-proportioned figure was revealed, his long fair hair held from his eyes by a silver coronet, his bronzed body clad in a short divided kilt of light brown color. He appeared to have no weapons.

Hawkmoon looked at him warily.

"Who are you?" he said. "What do you want?"

The occupant of the sphere smiled. "That's a question I should ask you," he said in a peculiar accent. "You have been in a fight, I see – and one of your number is dead. He seems old to have been a warrior."

"Who are you?" Hawkmoon asked again.

"You are single-minded, warrior. I am Zhenak-Teng of the family of Teng. Tell me who you fought here. Was it the Charki?"

"The name means nothing. We fought no one here," D'Averc said. "We are travellers. Those we fought are a great distance away now. We came here fleeing them . . ."

"And yet your wounds look fresh. You will accompany me back to Teng-Kampp?"

"That is your city?"

"We do not have cities. Come. We can help you – dress your wounds, perhaps even revive your friend."

"Impossible. He is dead."

"We can revive the dead as often as not," the handsome man said airily. "Will you come with me?"

Hawkmoon shrugged. "Why not?" He and D'Averc lifted the body of Mygan between them and advanced towards the sphere, Zhenak-Teng leading the way.

They saw that the interior of the sphere was, in fact, a cabin in which several men could sit comfortably. Doubtless the thing was a familiar form of transport here, for Zhenak-Teng made no effort to help them, leaving them to work out for themselves where they should sit and how they should position themselves.

He waved his hand over the control board of the sphere and the crack in the side began to seal itself. Then they were off, rolling smoothly over the turf at a fantastic speed, seeing dimly the landscape they passed.

The plain stretched on and on. Never once did they see trees or rocks or hills or rivers. Hawkmoon began to wonder if it were not, in fact, artificial – or had been artificially levelled at some time in the past.

Zhenak-Teng had his eyes pressed close to some instrument through which, presumably, he could see his way. His hands were on a lever attached to a wheel which he swung in one direction or another from time to time, doubtless steering the strange vehicle.

Once they passed at a distance a group of moving objects that they could not define through the shifting walls of the sphere. Hawkmoon pointed them out.

"Charki," Zhenak-Teng said. "With luck, they will not attack."

They seemed to be grey things, the color of dark stone, but with many legs and waving protuberances. Hawkmoon could not decide whether they were creatures or machines, or neither.

An hour passed and at last the sphere began to slow. "We are nearing Teng-Kampp," Zhenak-Teng said.

A little later the sphere rolled to a halt and the bronzed man leant back, sighing with relief. "Good," he said. "I found what I set out looking for. That force of Charki is feeding in a south-westerly direction and should not come too close to Teng-Kampp."

"What are the Charki?" D'Averc asked, gasping as he moved and his wounds began to hurt again.

"The Charki are our enemies, creatures created to destroy human life," Zhenak-Teng replied. "They feed from above ground, sucking up energy from the hidden Kampps of our people."

He touched a lever and with a jolt the globe began to descend into the ground.

The earth seemed to swallow them up and then close above them. The globe continued to descend for a few moments and then stopped. A bright light came on suddenly and they saw they were in a small underground chamber, barely large enough to hold the sphere.

"Teng-Kampp," said Zhenak-Teng laconically, touching a stud in the control panel which caused the sphere to split again.

They descended to the floor of the chamber, carrying Mygan with them, ducking to pass under an archway and emerge in another chamber where men dressed similarly to Zhenak-Teng hurried forward, presumably to service the sphere.

"This way," the tall man said, leading them into a cubicle which began to spin slowly. Hawkmoon and D'Averc leant against the sides of the cubicle, feeling dizzy, but at last the experience was over and Zhenak-Teng led them out into a richly carpeted room full of simple, comfortable looking furniture.

"These are my apartments," he said. "I'll send now for the medical members of my family who may be able to help your friend. Excuse me." He disappeared into another room.

A little later he came back smiling. "My brothers will be here soon."

"I hope so," said D'Averc fastidiously. "I've never been greatly fond of the company of corpses . . ."

"It will not be long. Come, let us go into another room where

83

refreshment awaits you."

They left the body of Mygan behind and entered a room where trays of food and drink seemed to drift, unsupported, in the air above piled cushions.

Following Zhenak-Teng's example, they seated themselves on the cushions and helped themselves to the food. It was delicious and they found themselves eating tremendous quantities of it.

As they ate, two men, of a similar appearance to Zhenak-Teng, entered the room.

"It is too late," said one of them to Zhenak-Teng. "I am sorry, brother, but we cannot revive the old man. The wounds, and the time involved . . ."

Zhenak-Teng looked apologetically at D'Averc and Hawkmoon. "There – you have lost your comrade for good, I fear."

"Then perhaps you can give him a good departure," said D'Averc, almost relieved.

"Of course. We shall do what is necessary."

The other two withdrew for about half-an-hour and then returned just as Hawkmoon and D'Averc finished eating. The first man introduced himself as Bralan-Teng and the second announced himself as Polad-Teng. They were both brothers to Zhenak-Teng and practitioners of medicine. They inspected Hawkmoon's and D'Averc's wounds and applied dressings. Very shortly the two men began to feel improved.

"Now you must tell me how you came to the land of the Kampps," Zhenak-Teng said. "We have few strangers on our plain, because of the Charki. You must tell me of events in the other parts of the world . . ."

"I am not sure that you would understand the answer to your first enquiry," Hawkmoon told him, "or that we can help you with news of our world." And he explained, as best he could, how they had come here and where their world was. Zhenak-Teng listened with careful attention.

"Aye," he said, "you are right. I can understand little of what you tell me. I have never heard of any 'Europe' or 'Granbretan' and the device you describe is not known to our science. But I believe you. How else could you have turned up so suddenly in the land of Kampps?"

"What are the Kampps?" D'Averc asked. "You said they were not cities."

"So they are not. They are family houses, belonging to one clan. In our case, the underground house belongs to the Teng family. Other nearby families are the Ohn, the Sek and the Neng. Years ago there were more – many more – but the Charki found them and destroyed them . . ."

"And what are the Charki?" Hawkmoon put it.

"The Charki are our age-old enemies. They were created by those who once sought to destroy the houses of the plain. That enemy destroyed himself, ultimately, with some kind of explosive experiment, but his creatures – the Charki – continue to wander the plain. They have unwholesome means of defeating us so that they may feed off our life-energy." Zhenak-Teng shuddered.

"They feed off your life-energy?" D'Averc said with a frown. "What is that?"

"Whatever gives us life – whatever life is, they take it and leave us drained, useless, dying slowly, unable to move . . ."

Hawkmoon began another question, then changed his mind. Evidently the subject was painful to Zhenak-Teng. Instead he asked, "And what is this plain? It does not seem natural to me."

"It is not. It was once the site of our landing fields, for we of the One Hundred Families were once mighty and powerful – until the coming of he who created the Charki. He wanted our artifacts and our sources of power for himself. He was called Shenatar-vron-Kensai and he brought the Charki with him from the east, their vocation being entirely to destroy the Families. And destroy them they did, save for the handful that still survives. But gradually, through the centuries, the Charki sniff them out . . ."

"You seem to have no hope," said D'Averc, almost accusingly.

"We are merely realistic," Zhenak-Teng replied without rancour.

"Tomorrow we should like to be on our way," said Hawkmoon. "Have you maps – something that will help us reach Narleen?"

"I have a map – though it is crude. Narleen used to be a great trading city on the coast. That was centuries ago. I do not know what it has become."

Zhenak-Teng rose. "I will show you to the room I have had prepared for you. There you may sleep tonight and begin your long journey in the morning."

85

Chapter Two
THE CHARKI

HAWKMOON AWOKE to the sounds of battle.

He wondered for a moment if he had dreamed and he was back in the cave and D'Averc was still engaged with Baron Meliadus. He sprang from his bed reaching for the sword that lay on a nearby stool with his tattered clothes. He was in the room where Zhenak-Teng had left them the previous night, and on the other bed D'Averc was awake, his features startled.

Hawkmoon began to struggle into his clothes. From behind the door came yells, the clash of swords, strange whining sounds and moans. When he was dressed, he went swiftly to the door and opened it a crack.

He was astonished. The bronzed, handsome folk of Teng-Kampp were busily at work trying to destroy one another – and it was not swords, after all, that were making the clashing sound, but meat cleavers, iron bars and a weird collection of domestic and scientific tools utilised as weapons. Snarls, bestial and alarming, were on all faces, and foam flecked lips, while eyes stared madly. Some insanity possessed them all!

Dark blue smoke began to pour along the corridor; there was a stink Hawkmoon could not define, the sound of smashing glass and torn metal.

"By the Runestaff, D'Averc," he gasped. "They seem possessed!"

A knot of battling men suddenly pressed against the door, pushing it inwards and Hawkmoon found himself in the middle of them. He pushed them back, sprang aside. None attacked him or D'Averc. They continued to butcher one another as if unaware of the spectators.

"This way," Hawkmoon said, and left the room, sword in hand. He coughed as the blue smoke entered his lungs and stung his eyes. Everywhere was ruin. Corpses lay thick in the corridor.

Together they struggled along the passages until they reached Zhenak-Teng's apartments. The door was locked. Frantically, Hawkmoon beat upon it with the pommel of his blade.

"Zhenak-Teng, it is Hawkmoon and D'Averc! Are you within?"

There was a movement from the other side of the door, then it sprang open and Zhenak-Teng, his eyes wild with terror, beckoned them in, then hastily closed and locked the door again.

"The Charki," he said. "There must have been another pack roaming elsewhere. I have failed in my duty. They took us by surprise. We are doomed."

"I see no monsters," D'Averc said. "Your kinsmen fight among themselves."

"Aye – that's the Charki's way of defeating us. They emit waves – mental rays of some description – that turn us mad, make us see enemies in our closest friends and brothers. And while we fight, they enter our Kampp. They will soon be here!"

"The blue smoke – what is that?" D'Averc asked.

"Nothing to do with the Charki. It comes from our smashed generators. We have no power now, even if we could rally."

From somewhere above came terrible thumps and crashes that shook the room.

"The Charki," murmured Zhenak-Teng. "Soon their rays will reach me, even me . . ."

"Why have they not reached you already?" Hawkmoon demanded.

"Some of us are more able to resist them. You, plainly, do not suffer from them at all. Others are quickly overcome."

"Can we not escape?" Hawkmoon glanced about the room. "The sphere we came in . . . ?"

"Too late, too late . . ."

D'Averc grasped Zhenak-Teng by the shoulder. "Come man, we can escape if we're quick. You can drive the sphere!"

"I must die with my family – the family I helped destroy." Zhenak-Teng was barely recognisable as the self-contained, civilised man they had spoken to the day before. All the spirit had left him. Already his eyes were glazed and it seemed to Hawkmoon that soon the man would succumb to the strange power of the Charki.

He came to a decision, raised his sword and struck swiftly. The pommel connected with the base of Zhenak-Teng's skull and he collapsed.

"Now, D'Averc," Hawkmoon said grimly. "Let's get him to the sphere. Hurry!"

Coughing as the blue smoke grew thicker, they stumbled from the room and into the passages, carrying Zhenak-Teng's unconscious body between them. Hawkmoon remembered the way to the place where they had left the sphere and directed D'Averc.

Now the whole passage shook alarmingly until they were forced to stop to keep their balance. Then . . .

"The wall! It's crumbling!" howled D'Averc, staggering back. "Quickly, Hawkmoon – the other way!"

"We must get to the sphere!" Hawkmoon called back. "We must go on!"

Now pieces of the ceiling began to fall and a grey, stone-like thing crept through the crack in the wall and into the passage. On the end of the thing was what resembled a sucker such as an octopus would possess, moving like a mouth seeking to kiss them.

Hawkmoon shuddered in horror and stabbed at the thing with his sword. It recoiled, then, pouting a little, as if only a trifle offended by his gesture and willing to make friends, it advanced again.

This time Hawkmoon chopped at it and there was a grunt and a shrill hiss from the other side of the room. The creature seemed surprised that something was resisting it. Heaving Zhenak-Teng onto his shoulder, Hawkmoon struck another blow at the tentacle, then leapt over it and began to race down the crumbling passage.

"Come on, D'Averc! To the sphere!"

D'Averc skipped over the wounded tentacle and followed. Now the wall gave way altogether, and it revealed a mass of waving arms, a pulsing head and a face that was a parody of human features, grinning a placatory, idiot's grin.

"It wants us to pet it!" D'Averc cried with grim humor as he avoided a reaching tentacle. "Would you hurt its feelings so, Hawkmoon?"

Hawkmoon was busily opening the door that led to the chamber of the sphere. Zhenak-Teng, who lay on the floor near him, was beginning to moan and clutch his head.

Hawkmoon got the door open, hefted Zhenak-Teng onto his shoulder again, and passed through into the chamber where the sphere lay.

No noise came from it now and its colors were muted, but it was opened sufficient to admit them. Hawkmoon climbed the ladder and dumped Zhenak-Teng in the control seat as D'Averc joined him.

"Get this thing moving," he told Zhenak-Teng, "or we'll all be devoured by the Charki you see there . . . " He pointed with his sword to the giant thing that was squeezing its way through the door of the chamber.

Several tentacles crept up the sides of the sphere towards them. One touched Zhenak-Teng lightly on the shoulder and he moaned. Hawkmoon yelled and chopped at it. It flopped to the floor. But others were now waving all around him and had fastened on the bronzed man who seemed to accept the touch with complete passivity. Hawkmoon and D'Averc screamed at him to get the sphere moving while they hacked desperately at the dozens of waving limbs.

Hawkmoon reached out with his left hand to grasp the back of Zhenak-Teng's neck. "Close the sphere, Zhenak-Teng! Close the sphere."

With a jerky movement, Zhenak-Teng obeyed, depressing a stud which made the sphere murmur and hum and begin to glow with all kinds of colors.

The tentacles tried to resist the steady motion of the walls as the aperture closed. Three leapt through D'Averc's defense and fastened themselves on Zhenak-Teng who groaned and went limp. Again Hawkmoon slashed at the tentacles as the sphere finally closed and began to rise upwards.

One by one the tentacles disappeared as the sphere rose and Hawkmoon sighed in relief. He turned to the bronzed man. "We are free!"

But Zhenak-Teng stared dully ahead of him, his arms limp at his sides.

"It is no good," he said slowly. "It has taken my life . . ." And he slumped to one side, falling to the floor.

Hawkmoon bent beside him, putting his hand to the man's chest to feel his heartbeat. He shuddered in horror.

"He's cold, D'Averc – incredibly cold!"

"And does he live?" the Frenchman asked.

Hawkmoon shook his head. "He is entirely dead."

The sphere was still rising rapidly and Hawkmoon sprang to the controls, looking at them in despair, not knowing one instrument from another, not daring to touch anything lest they descend again to where the Charki feasted on the life energy of the people of Teng-Kampp.

Suddenly they were in the open air and bounding over the turf. Hawkmoon seated himself in the control seat and took the lever as he had seen Zhenak-Teng take it the day before. Gingerly he pushed it to one side, and had the satisfaction of seeing the sphere begin to roll in that direction.

"I think I can steer it," he told his friend. "But how one stops it or opens it, that I cannot guess!"

"As long as we are leaving those monsters behind, I am not entirely depressed," D'Averc said with a smile. "Turn the thing to the south, Hawkmoon. At least we will be going in the direction we intended."

Hawkmoon did as D'Averc suggested and for hours they rolled over the flat plain until, at length, a forest came in sight.

"It will be interesting," said D'Averc, when Hawkmoon pointed out the trees to him, "to see how the sphere behaves when it reaches the trees. It was plainly not designed for such terrain."

Chapter Three
THE SAYOU RIVER

THE SPHERE STRUCK the trees with a great sound of snapping wood and tortured metal.

D'Averc and Hawkmoon found themselves flung to the far side of the control chamber, keeping company with the unpleasantly cold corpse of Zhenak-Teng.

Next they were flung upwards, then sideways, and had not

90

the walls of the sphere been well padded, they would have died of broken bones.

At last the sphere rolled to a halt, rocked for a few moments, then suddenly split apart, tumbling Hawkmoon and D'Averc to the ground.

D'Averc groaned. "What an unnecessary experience for one so weak as myself."

Hawkmoon grinned, partly at his friend's drollery, partly in relief.

"Well," he said, "we have escaped more easily than I'd dared hope. Rise up, D'Averc, we must strike on – strike for the South!"

"I think a rest is called for," D'Averc said, stretching and looking up at the green branches of the trees. Sun slanted through them, turning the forest to emerald and gold. There was the sharp scent of pine and the earthier scent of the birch and from a branch above them a squirrel looked down, its bright black eyes sardonic. Behind them the wreckage of the sphere lay amongst tangled roots and branches. Several small trees had been torn up and others snapped. Hawkmoon realised that their escape had been very lucky indeed. He began to shake, now, with reaction, and understood the sense of D'Averc's words. He sat down on a grassy hillock, averting his eyes from the wreck and the corpse of Zhenak-Teng that could just be seen to one side of the sphere.

D'Averc lay down nearby and rolled over onto his back. From within his tattered jerkin he drew a tightly wadded piece of parchment, the map that Zhenak-Teng had given him shortly before they retired the night before.

D'Averc opened the parchment and studied it. It showed the plain in considerable detail, marked the various Kampps of Zhenak-Teng's people and what appeared to be the hunting trails of the Charki. Against most of the sites of the underground dwellings were crosses, presumably showing which the Charki had destroyed.

He pointed to a spot near the corner of the map. "Here," he said. "Here's the forest – and just to the north here is marked a river – the Sayou. This arrow points south to Narleen. From what I can gather, the river will lead us to the city."

Hawkmoon nodded. "Then let's head for the river when we're recovered. The sooner we reach Narleen, the better – for there at least we may discover where we are in space and time. It was unlucky that the Charki should have attacked when they did. By questioning Zhenak-Teng longer, we might have been able to learn from him where we were."

They slept in the peace of the forest for an hour or more, then rose up, adjusted their worn gear and ragged clothes, and set off towards the north and the river.

As they progressed, the undergrowth grew thicker and the trees more dense, and the hills on which the trees clung became steeper, so that by evening they were weary and in ill-temper, barely speaking to one another.

Hawkmoon sorted through the few objects in the purse on his belt, found a tinder box of ornate design. They walked on for another half-hour until they came to a stream that fed a pool set between high banks on three sides. Beside this was a small clearing and Hawkmoon said: "'We'll spend the night here, D'Averc, for I cannot continue any longer."

D'Averc nodded and flung himself down beside the pool, drinking greedily the clear water. "It looks deep," he said, rising and wiping his lips.

Hawkmoon was building a fire and did not reply.

Soon he had a good blaze going.

"We should, perhaps, hunt for game," D'Averc said lazily. "I am becoming hungry. Do you know anything of forest lore, Hawkmoon?"

"Some," said Hawkmoon, "but I am not hungry, D'Averc."

And with that he lay down and went to sleep.

It was night, it was cold, and Hawkmoon was suddenly awakened by a terrified yell from his friend.

He was up instantly, staring in the direction D'Averc pointed, sword leaping from his scabbard. He gasped in horror at what he saw.

Rising from the waters of the pool, water rushing from its huge sides, was a reptilian creature with blazing black eyes and scales as black as the night. Only its mouth, which now gaped wide, contained the whiteness of pointed teeth. With a great slopping sound it was heaving itself through the water toward them.

Hawkmoon staggered back, feeling dwarfed by the monster.

Its head darted down and forward, its jaws snapping inches from his face, its loathsome breath almost asphyxiating him.

"Run, Hawkmoon, run!" yelled D'Averc, and together they began to stumble back into the woods.

But the creature was out of the water now and giving chase. From its throat came a terrible croaking noise that seemed to fill the forest. Hawkmoon and D'Averc clutched at one another's hands to keep together as they stumbled through the undergrowth, almost blind in the blackness of the night.

Again the croaking noise and this time a long, soft tongue whistled like a whip through the air and encircled D'Averc's waist.

D'Averc screamed and slashed at the tongue with his blade. Hawkmoon yelled and sprang forward, stabbing out at the black thing with all his might, while hanging to D'Averc's hand and holding his ground as best he could.

Inexorably, the tongue drew them towards the gaping mouth of the water-beast. Hawkmoon could see that it was hopeless to try to save D'Averc in this way. He let go of D'Averc's hand and leapt to one side, slashing at the thick, black tongue.

Then he took his sword in both hands, raised it above his head and chopped down with all his strength.

The beast croaked again and the ground shook, but the tongue parted slowly and foul blood gushed from it. Then there came a hideous cry and the trees began to part and snap as the water-thing lumbered at them. Hawkmoon grabbed D'Averc and hauled him to his feet, pushing aside the sticky flesh of the severed tongue.

"Thanks," D'Averc panted as they ran. "I'm beginning to dislike this land, Hawkmoon – it seems more full of perils than our own!"

Crunching and croaking and crying out with insensate rage, the thing from the pool pursued them.

"It's nearly on us again!" shouted Hawkmoon. "We can't escape it!"

They turned, peering through the blackness. All they could see now were the two blazing black eyes of the creature. Hawkmoon hefted his sword in his hand, getting its balance. 'There's only one chance," he called, and flung his sword straight at the malevolent eyes.

There was another croaking scream and a great threshing

sound amongst the trees, then the blazing orbs disappeared and they heard the beast crashing away, back to the pool.

Hawkmoon gasped with relief. "I didn't kill it, but it doubtless decided we were not the easy prey it originally took us for. Come, D'Averc, let's get to that river as soon as we can. I want to leave this forest behind!"

"And what makes you think the river is any less perilous?" D'Averc asked him sardonically as they began to move through the forest again, taking their direction from the side of the trees on which moss grew.

Two days later they broke out of the forest and stood on the sides of a hill that went steeply down to a valley through which a broad river flowed. It was without doubt the River Sayou.

They were covered in filth, unshaven, their clothes ragged to the point of disintegration. Hawkmoon had only a dagger for a weapon, and D'Averc, at last rid of his torn jerkin, was naked to the waist.

They ran down the hill, stumbling over roots, struck by branches, careless of any discomfort in their haste to reach the river.

Where the river would take them, they knew not, but they wished now only to leave the forest and its monsters for, though they had encountered nothing as dreadful as the creature from the pool, they had seen other monsters from a distance, discovered the spoor of still others.

They flung themselves into the water and began to wash the mud and filth from their bodies, grinning at one another.

"Ah, sweet water!" exclaimed D'Averc. "You lead to towns and cities and civilisation. I care not what that civilisation offers us – it will be more familiar and even more welcome than the worst this dirty *natural* place presents to us!"

Hawkmoon smiled, not entirely sharing D'Averc's sentiments, but understanding his feelings.

"We'll build a raft," he said. "We're lucky that the current flows south. All we need do, D'Averc, is let the current bear us to our goal!"

"And you can fish, Hawkmoon – get us tasty meals. I'm not used to the simple fare we've lived on the past two days – berries and roots, ugh!"

"I'll teach you how to fish, too, D'Averc. The experience

might be useful to you if you find yourself in a similar situation in the future!" And Hawkmoon laughed, slapping his friend on the back.

Chapter Four
VALJON OF STARVEL

FOUR DAYS LATER the raft had borne them many miles down the great river. Forests no longer lined the banks, but instead there were gentle hills and seas of wild corn on both sides of them.

Hawkmoon and D'Averc lived off the fat fish they caught in the river, together with corn and fruit found on the banks, and they became more relaxed as the raft drifted on toward Narleen.

They had the appearance of shipwrecked sailors, with their ragged clothes and beards that grew thicker daily, but their eyes no longer had the wild look of hunger and exposure and they were in better spirits than they had been.

It was late in the afternoon of the fourth day that they saw the ship and leapt to their feet to wave wildly in an attempt to attract its attention.

"Perhaps the ship is from Narleen!" cried Hawkmoon. "Perhaps they'll let us work a passage to the city!"

The ship was high-prowed, made of wood painted with rich colors. Principally it was red, with gold, yellow and blue scroll-work along its sides. Although rigged like a two-masted schooner it also possessed oars which were now being used to propel it against the current toward them. It flew a hundred brightly colored flags and the men on its decks wore clothes to match.

The ship struck her oars and pulled alongside. A heavily bearded face peered down at them. "Who are you?"

"Travellers – strangers in these parts – can we sign aboard to work our passage to Narleen?" D'Averc asked.

The bearded man laughed. "Aye, that you can. Come up, gentlemen."

A rope ladder was thrown down and Hawkmoon and D'Averc climbed gratefully up it to stand on the ornamental deck of the ship.

"This is the *River Hawk*," the bearded man told them. "Heard of her?"

"I told you – we're strangers," said Hawkmoon.

"Aye . . . Well, she's owned by Valjon of Starvel – you've heard of *him* no doubt."

"No," said D'Averc. "But we're grateful to him for sending a ship our way," he smiled. "Now, my friend, what do you say to our working our passage to Narleen?"

"Well, if you've no money . . ."

"None . . ."

"We'd best find out from Valjon himself what he wants done with you."

The bearded man escorted them up the deck to the poop where a thin man stood brooding, not looking at them.

"Lord Valjon?" said the bearded man.

"What is it, Ganak?"

"The two we took aboard. They've no money – wish to work their passage, they say."

"Why, then let them, Ganak, if that's what they desire." Valjon smiled wanly. "Let them."

He did not look directly at Hawkmoon and D'Averc and his melancholy eyes continued to stare out over the river. With a wave of his hand he dismissed them.

Hawkmoon felt uncomfortable, looked about him. All the crew were looking on silently, faint smiles on their faces. "What's the joke?" he said, for plainly there was one.

"Joke?" Ganak said. "There's none. Now, gentlemen, would you pull an oar to get you to Narleen?"

"If that's the work that will get us to the city," said D'Averc with some reluctance.

"It looks somewhat strenuous work," Hawkmoon said. "But it's not too far to Narleen, if our map was in order. Show us to our oars, friend Ganak."

Ganak took them along the deck until they reached the catwalk between the rowers. Here Hawkmoon was shocked when he saw the condition of the oarsmen. All looked half-starved and filthy. "I don't understand . . ." he began.

Ganak laughed. "Why, you will soon."

"What are these rowers?" D'Averc asked in dismay.

"They are slaves, *gentlemen* – and slaves you are, too. We take nothing aboard the *River Hawk* that will not profit us and, since you have no money, and ransom seems unlikely, why we'll make you slaves to work our oars for us. Get down there!"

D'Averc drew his sword and Hawkmoon his dagger, but Ganak sprang back signalling to his crewmen. "Take them, lads. Teach them new tricks, for they seem not to understand what slaves must do."

Behind them, along the catwalk, clambered a great weight of sailors, all with bright blades in their hands, while another mass of men came at their front.

D'Averc and Hawkmoon prepared to die taking a good quantity of the sailors with them, but then from above a figure came hurtling, down a rope from the crosstrees, to strike once, twice upon their heads with a hardwood club and knock them into the oarpits.

The figure grinned and bounced on the catwalk, putting away his club. Ganak laughed and clapped him on the shoulder. "Good work, Orindo. That trick's always the best one and saves much spilt blood."

Others sprang down to relieve the stunned men of their weapons and rope their wrists to an oar.

When Hawkmoon awoke, he and D'Averc sat side by side on a hard bench and Orindo was swinging his legs from the catwalk above them. He was a boy of perhaps sixteen, a cocky smile on his face.

He called back to someone above whom they could not see. "They're awake. We can start moving now – back to Narleen."

He winked at Hawkmoon and D'Averc. "Commence, gentlemen," he said, "Commence rowing, if you please." He seemed to be imitating a voice he had heard. "You're lucky," he added. "We're turning downstream. Your first work will be easy."

Hawkmoon gave a mock bow over his oar. "Thank you, young man. We appreciate your concern."

"I'll give you further advice from time to time, for that's my kindly nature," said Orindo springing up, gathering his red and blue coat about him and bouncing along the catwalk.

Ganak's face peered down next. He prodded at Hawkmoon's shoulder with a sharp boathook. "Pull well, friend, or you'll feel the bite of this in your bowels." Ganak disappeared. The other rowers bent to their task and Hawkmoon and D'Averc were forced to follow suit.

For the best part of a day they pulled, with the stink of their own and others' bodies in their nostrils, with a bowl of slops to eat at midday. The work was backbreaking, though it was a sign of what upstream rowing was like when the other slaves murmured with gratitude for the ease of their task!

At night, they lay over their oars, barely able to eat their second bowl of nauseating mess that was, if anything, worse then the first.

Hawkmoon and D'Averc were too weary to talk, but made some attempt to rid themselves of their bonds. It was impossible for they were too weak to get free of such tightly knotted ropes.

Next morning Ganak's voice awoke them. "All port rowers get pulling. Come on you, scum! That means you, gentlemen! Pull! Pull! There's a prize in sight and if we miss it, you'll suffer the Lord Valjon's wrath!"

The emaciated bodies of the other rowers instantly became active at this threat and Hawkmoon and D'Averc bent their backs with them, hauling the huge boat round against the current.

From above were the sounds of footfalls as men rushed about, preparing the ship for battle. Ganak's voice roared from the poop as he issued instructions in the name of his master, the Lord Valjon.

Hawkmoon thought he would die with the effort of rowing, felt his heart pound and his muscles creak with the agony of the exertion. Fit he might be, but this effort was unusual, placing strain on parts of his body that had never had to take such strain before. He was covered in sweat and his hair was pasted to his face, his mouth open as he gasped for breath.

"Oh, Hawkmoon . . ." panted D'Averc. "This – was – not – meant to – be – my role – in life . . ."

But Hawkmoon could not reply for the pain in his chest and arms.

There was now a sharp jarring as the boat met another

and Ganak yelled: "Port rowers, drop oars!"

Hawkmoon and the others obeyed instantly and slumped over their oars as the sounds of battle commenced above. There was the noise of swords, of men in agony, of killing and of dying, but it seemed only like a distant dream to Hawkmoon. He felt that if he continued to row in Lord Valjon's galley, he would shortly die.

Then suddenly he heard a guttural cry above him and felt a great weight fall upon him. The thing struggled, crawled over his head, then fell in front of him. It was a brutish looking sailor, his body covered in red hair. There was a large cutlass sticking from the middle of his body. He gasped, quivered, then died, the knife falling from his hand.

Hawkmoon stared at him dully for a while, then his brain began to work. He extended his feet and found he could touch the fallen knife. Gradually, with several pauses, he drew it towards him until it was under his bench. Then, exhausted, he again fell over his oar.

Meanwhile the sounds of fighting died down and Hawkmoon was recalled to reality by the smell of burning timber, looked about him in panic, then realised the truth.

"It's the other ship that's burning," D'Averc told him. "We're aboard a pirate, friend Hawkmoon. A pirate." He smiled sardonically. "What an unworthy occupation – and my health so frail . . ."

Hawkmoon reflected, with some self-judgement, that D'Averc seemed to be reacting better to their situation than was he.

He drew a deep breath and straightened his shoulders as best he could.

"I have a knife . . ." he began in a whisper. But D'Averc nodded rapidly.

"I know. I saw you. Quick thinking, Hawkmoon. You're not in such bad condition, after all. Why, I thought you expired until recently!"

Hawkmoon said: "Rest tonight, until just before dawn. Then we'll escape."

"Aye," agreed D'Averc. "We'll save as much strength as we can. Courage, Hawkmoon – we'll soon be free men again!"

For the rest of the day they pulled rapidly downriver, pausing only at noon for their bowl of slops. Once Ganak squatted on the catwalk and tickled Hawkmoon's shoulder with his boat-hook.

"Well, my friends, another day and you'll have your desire. We'll be docking at Starvel tomorrow."

"And what's Starvel?" croaked Hawkmoon.

Ganak looked at him astonished. "You must be from far away if you've not heard of Starvel. It's part of Narleen – the most favored part. The walled city where the great princes of the river dwell – and of whom Lord Valjon is the greatest."

"Are they all pirates?" asked D'Averc.

"Careful, stranger," Ganak said frowning. "We help ourselves by right to whatever's on the river. The river belongs to Lord Valjon and his peers."

He straightened up and strode away. They rowed on until nightfall and then, at Ganak's order, ceased their work. Hawkmoon had found the work easier, now that his muscles and body had become used to it, but he was still tired.

"We must sleep in shifts," he murmured to D'Averc as they ate their slops. "You first, then I."

D'Averc nodded and slumped down almost instantly.

The night grew cold, and Hawkmoon could barely stop from falling asleep himself. He heard the first watch sounded, then the second. With relief, he nudged at D'Averc until he was awake.

D'Averc grunted and Hawkmoon was asleep, remembering D'Averc's words. By dawn, with luck, they would be free. Then would come the difficult part – of leaving the ship unseen.

He awoke feeling strangely light in the body and realised with mounting spirits that his hands were free of the oars. D'Averc must have worked in the night. It was almost dawn.

He turned to his friend who grinned at him and winked. "Ready?" D'Averc murmured.

"Aye . . ." replied Hawkmoon with a great sigh. He looked with envy at the long knife D'Averc held.

"If I had a weapon," he said, "I would repay Ganak for a few indignities . . ."

"No time for that now," D'Averc pointed out. "We must escape as silently as possible."

Cautiously they rose up from the benches and poked their heads up over the catwalk. At the far end, a sailor stood on watch, and on the poop deck, his posture brooding and abstracted, stood Lord Valjon, his pale face staring into the darkness of the river night.

The sailor's back was towards them and Valjon did not seem ready to turn. The two men heaved themselves onto the catwalk, making stealthily for the prow of the ship.

But it was then that Valjon turned, then that his sepulchral voice spoke.

"What's this? Two slaves escaping?"

Hawkmoon shuddered. The man's instinct was uncanny, for it was plain he had not seen them, perhaps had only heard them for a moment. His voice, though deep and quiet, somehow carried the length of the ship. The sailor on watch turned and yelled. Above him now, Lord Valjon's head turned and the deathly pale face glared at them.

From below decks several sailors appeared, blocking their way to the side. They wheeled and Hawkmoon began to run toward the poop and Lord Valjon. The sailor drew his cutlass and struck at him, but Hawkmoon was desperate. He ducked beneath the blow, grasped the man by the waist and heaved him up to hurl him to the deck where he lay winded. Instantly Hawkmoon, too long tired of inaction, picked up the unwieldy blade and struck off the man's head. Then he turned to stare up at Lord Valjon.

The pirate lord seemed undisturbed by the closeness of danger. He continued to stare at Hawkmoon from his pale, bleak eyes.

"You are a fool," he said slowly. "For I am the Lord Valjon."

"And I am Dorian Hawkmoon, Duke von Köln! I have fought and defeated the Dark Lords of Granbretan, have resisted their most powerful magic as this stone in my skull testifies. I do not fear you, Lord Valjon, the pirate!"

"Then fear those," murmured Valjon, pointing a bony finger behind Hawkmoon.

Hawkmoon spun on his heel and saw a great number of sailors bearing down on him and D'Averc. And D'Averc was armed only with a knife.

Hawkmoon flung him the cutlass. "Hold them off, D'Averc. I'll take their leader!" And he leapt for the poop, grasped the rail and hauled himself over it as Lord Valjon, an expression of mild surprise on his face, took a step or two backward.

Hawkmoon advanced toward him, hands outstretched.

From under his loose robe Valjon drew a slim blade which he pointed at Hawkmoon, making no attempt to attack but backing away.

"Slave," murmured Lord Valjon, his grim features baffled. "Slave."

"I'm no slave, as you'll discover." Hawkmoon ducked past the blade and tried to grab the strange pirate captain. Valjon stepped aside swiftly, still keeping the long sword before him.

Evidently Hawkmoon's attack on him was unprecedented, for Valjon hardly knew what to do. He had been disturbed from some brooding trance and stared at Hawkmoon as if he were not real.

Hawkmoon leapt again, avoiding the extended sword. Again Valjon sidestepped.

Below, D'Averc had his back to the poop deck, was just able to hold off the sailors who crammed the narrow catwalk. He called up to Hawkmoon:

"Hurry up with your business, friend Hawkmoon – or I'll have a dozen skewers in me before long!"

Hawkmoon aimed a blow at Valjon's face, felt his fist connect with cold, dry flesh, saw the man's head snap back and the sword fall from his hand. Hawkmoon swept up the sword, admiring its balance, and heaved the unconscious Valjon to his feet, directing the sword at his vitals.

"Back, scum, or your master dies!" He yelled. "Back!"

In astonishment the sailors began to back away, leaving three of their number dead at D'Averc's feet. Ganak came hurrying up behind them. He was wearing only a kilt, a naked cutlass in his hand. His jaw dropped when he saw Hawkmoon.

"Now, D'Averc, perhaps you'd care to join me up here," Hawkmoon called almost merrily.

D'Averc circled the poop and climbed the ladder to the deck. He grinned at Hawkmoon. "Good work, friend."

"We'll wait until dawn!" Hawkmoon called. "And then you sailors will direct this ship to the shore. When that's done, and we're free, perhaps I'll let your master go alive."

Ganak scowled. "You are a fool to handle Lord Valjon thus. Know you not that he is the most powerful river prince in Starvel."

"I know nothing of your Starvel, friend, but I have dared the dangers of Granbretan, have ventured into the Dark Empire's very heart, and I doubt if you can offer dangers more sophisticated than theirs. Fear is an emotion I rarely feel, Ganak. But mark you this – I would be revenged on you. Your days are numbered."

Ganak laughed. "Your luck makes you stupid, slave! Vengeance-taking will be the Lord Valjon's prerogative!"

Dawn was already beginning to lighten the horizon. Hawkmoon ignored Ganak's jibe.

It seemed a century before the sun finally rose and began to dapple the distant trees of the riverbank. They were anchored close to the left bank of the river, not far from a small cove that could just be made out about half a mile away.

"Give the order to row, Ganak!" Hawkmoon called. "Make for the left shore."

Ganak scowled and made no effort to obey.

Hawkmoon's arm encircled Valjon's throat. The man was beginning to blink awake. Hawkmoon tapped his stomach with his sword. "Ganak! I could make Valjon die slowly!"

Suddenly, from the throat of the pirate lord there came a tiny, ironic chuckle. "Die slowly . . ." he said. "Die slowly . . ."

Hawkmoon stared at him, puzzled. "Aye – I know where best to strike to give you the maximum time and maximum pain a-dying."

Valjon made no other sound, merely stood passively with his throat still gripped by Hawkmoon's arm.

"Now, Ganak! Give the instructions!" D'Averc called.

Ganak took a deep breath. "Rowers!" he cried, and began to issue orders. The oars creaked, the backs of the oarsmen bent, and slowly the ship began to ride toward the left bank of the wide Sayou River.

Hawkmoon watched Ganak closely, for fear the man would attempt to trick them, but Ganak did not move, merely scowled.

As the bank came closer and closer, Hawkmoon began to relax. They were almost free. On land they could avoid any pursuit by the sailors who would, anyway, doubtless be reluctant to leave their ship.

Then he heard D'Averc yell and point upward. He stared up to see a figure come whizzing down a rope above his head.

It was the boy Orindo, a hardwood club in his hand, a wild grin on his lips.

Hawkmoon released Valjon and raised his arms to protect himself, unable to do the obvious thing which was to use his blade to strike Orindo as he descended. The club fell heavily on his arm and he staggered back. D'Averc rushed forward and grasped Orindo round the waist, imprisoning his arms.

Valjon, suddenly swift-footed, darted down the companionway screaming a strange, wordless scream.

D'Averc pushed Orindo after him with an oath.

"Taken by the same trick twice, Hawkmoon. We deserve to die for that!"

Growling sailors led by Ganak were coming up the companionway now. Hawkmoon struck out at Ganak, but the bearded sailor blocked the blow, aiming a huge swing at Hawkmoon's legs. Hawkmoon was forced to leap back and then Ganak scuttled up to the poop and faced him, a sneering grin on his lips.

"Now, slave, we'll see how you fight a man!" Ganak said.

"I do not see a man," Hawkmoon replied. "Only some kind of beast." And he laughed as Ganak struck at him again, thrusting swiftly with the marvellously balanced sword he had taken from Valjon.

Back and forth across the deck they fought, while D'Averc managed to hold the others at bay. Ganak was a master swordsman, but his cutlass was no match for the shining sword of the pirate lord.

Hawkmoon took him in the shoulder with a darting thrust, reeled back as the cutlass collided with the hilt of his blade, feeling the weapon almost fall from his hand, recovered himself to thrust again and wound Ganak in the left arm.

The bearded man howled like an animal and came on with renewed ferocity.

Hawkmoon thrust again, this time wounding Ganak's right arm. Blood now drenched both brawny arms and Hawkmoon was unwounded. Ganak flung himself at Hawkmoon again, now in a kind of fierce panic.

Hawkmoon's next thrust was to the heart, to put Ganak out of further misery. The point of the blade bit through flesh, scraped against bone, and the life was gone from Ganak.

But now the other sailors had forced D'Averc back and he was surrounded, hacking about him with the cutlass. Hawkmoon left the corpse of Ganak and leapt forward, taking one in the throat and another under the ribs before they were aware of his presence.

Back to back now, Hawkmoon and D'Averc held off the sailors, but it seemed they must soon expire for more were running to join their comrades.

Soon the poop was heaped with corpses and Hawkmoon and D'Averc covered with cuts from a dozen blades, their bodies all bloody. Still they fought. Hawkmoon caught a glimpse of the Lord Valjon standing by the mainmast watching from out of his deepset eyes, staring fixedly at him as if he wished to have a clear impression of his face for the rest of his life if need be.

Hawkmoon shuddered, then returned his full attention to the attacking seamen. The flat of a cutlass caught him a blow on the head and he reeled against D'Averc, sending his friend off-balance. Together they collapsed to the deck, struggled to rise up, still fighting. Hawkmoon took one man in the stomach, struck another's lowering face with his fist, heaved himself to his knees.

Then suddenly the sailors stepped back, their eyes fixed to port. Hawkmoon sprang up, D'Averc with him.

The sailors were watching in concern as a new ship came swimming from the cove, its white, schooner-rigged sails billowing with the fresh breeze from the south, its rich black and deep blue paint all agleaming in the early morning sunshine, its sides lined with armed men.

"A rival pirate, no doubt," D'Averc said, and used his advantage to cut down the nearest sailor and run for the rail of the poop. Hawkmoon followed his example and, with backs pressed against the rail they fought on, though half their enemies were running down the companionway to present themselves to Lord Valjon for his orders.

A voice called across the water, but it was too far away for the words to be clear.

Somehow in the confusion, Hawkmoon heard Valjon's deep, world-weary voice speak a single word, a word containing much loathing.

The word was "Bewchard!"

Then the sailors were upon them again and Hawkmoon felt a cutlass nick his face, turned blazing eyes on his attacker and thrust out his sword to catch him through the mouth, driving the sharp blade upwards for the brain, hearing the man scream a long, horrible scream as he died.

Hawkmoon felt no mercy, yanked his sword back and stabbed another in the heart.

And thus they fought, while the black and midnight blue schooner sailed closer and closer.

For a moment, Hawkmoon wondered if the ship would be friend or foe. Then there was no more time for wondering as the vengeful sailors pressed in, their heavy cutlasses rising and falling.

Chapter Five
PAHL BEWCHARD

As the black and blue ship crashed alongside, Hawkmoon heard Valjon's voice calling.

"Forget the slaves! Forget them! Stand by to hold off Bewchard's dogs!"

The remaining sailors backed warily away from the panting Hawkmoon and D'Averc. Hawkmoon made a thrust at them that sent them away faster, but he had not the energy to pursue them for the moment.

They watched as sailors, all dressed in jerkins and hose that matched the paint of the ship, came sailing on ropes to land on the deck of the *River Hawk*. They were armed with heavy war-axes and sabres and fought with a precision that the pirates could not imitate, though they did their best to rally.

Hawkmoon looked for Lord Valjon, but he had disappeared – probably below decks.

He turned to D'Averc. "Well, we've done our share of blood-letting this day, my friend. What say you to a less lethal action – we could free the poor wretches at the oars!" And with that he leapt the poop rail to land on the catwalk and lean down to slash the knotted ropes binding the slaves to their oars.

They looked up in surprise, not realising, most of them, what Hawkmoon and D'Averc were doing for them.

"You're free," Hawkmoon told them.

"Free," D'Averc repeated. "Take our advice and leave the ship while you can, for there's no knowing how the battle will go."

The slaves stood up, stretching their aching limbs, and then, one by one, they hauled themselves to the side of the ship and began to slide into the water.

D'Averc watched them go with a grin.

"A shame we can't help those on the other side," he said.

"Why not?" asked Hawkmoon indicating a hatch let into the side under the catwalk. "If I'm not mistaken, this leads under the deck."

He put his back to the side of the ship and kicked at the hatch. Several kicks and it sprang open. They entered the darkness and crept under the boards, hearing the sounds of fighting immediately above them.

D'Averc paused, slicing open a bundle with his much-blunted blade. Jewels poured out of the bundle. "Their loot," he said.

"No time for that now," Hawkmoon warned, but D'Averc was grinning.

"I didn't plan to keep it," he told his friend, "but I'd hate Valjon to escape with it if the fight goes well for him. Look . . ." and he indicated a large circular object set into the bottom of the hold. "If I'm not mistaken, this will let a little of the river into the ship, my friend!"

Hawkmoon nodded. "While you work on that, I'll make haste to free the slaves."

He left D'Averc to his task and reached the far hatch, stripping out the pegs that held it in position.

The hatch burst inwards, bringing two struggling men with it. One wore the uniform of the attacking ship, the other was a pirate. With a quick movement, Hawkmoon despatched the pirate. The uniformed man looked at him in surprise. "You're one of the men we saw fighting on the poop deck!"

Hawkmoon nodded. "What's your ship?"

"It's Bewchard's ship," replied the man wiping his forehead, he spoke as if the name were sufficient explanation.

"And who is Bewchard?"

The uniformed man laughed. "Why, he's Valjon's sworn enemy, if that's what you need to know. He saw you fighting, too, was impressed by your swordsmanship."

"So he should have been," grinned Hawkmoon, "for I fought my best today. And why not? I was fighting for my life!"

"That often makes excellent swordsmen of us all," agreed the man. "I'm Culard – and your friend if you're Valjon's foe."

"Best warn your comrades, then," said Hawkmoon. "We're sinking the ship – look." He pointed through the dimness to where D'Averc was wrestling with the circular bung.

Culard nodded swiftly and ducked out into the slave pit again. "I'll see you after this is over, friend," he called as he left. "If we live!"

Hawkmoon followed him, creeping along the aisle to cut the slaves' bonds.

Above him the men of Bewchard's ship seemed to be driving Valjon's pirates back. Hawkmoon felt the ship move suddenly, saw D'Averc come hastily out of the hatch.

"I think we'd best make for the shore," said the Frenchman with a smile, jerking his thumb at the slaves who were disappearing over the side, "follow our friends' example."

Hawkmoon nodded. "I've warned Bewchard's men of what's happening. We've repaid Valjon now, I think." He tucked Valjon's sword under his arm. "I'll try not to lose this blade – it's the finest I've ever used. Such a blade would make an outstanding swordsman of anyone!"

He clambered up to the side and saw that Bewchard's men had driven the pirate sailors back to the other side of the ship but were now withdrawing.

Culard had evidently spread the news.

Water was bubbling through the hatch. The ship would not last long afloat. Hawkmoon turned and looked back. There was barely space between the ships to swim. The best method of escape would be to cross the deck of Bewchard's schooner.

He informed D'Averc of his plan. His friend nodded and they poised themselves on the rail, leaping out to land on the deck of the other ship.

There were no rowers present and Hawkmoon realized that Bewchard's oarsmen must be free men, part of the fighting complement of the ship. This, it seemed to him, was a more sensible scheme – less wasteful than the use of slaves. It also gave him cause to pause and, as he paused, a voice called from the *River Hawk*.

"Hey, my friend. You with the black gem in your forehead.

Have you plans for scuttling my ship, too?"

Hawkmoon turned and saw a good looking young man, dressed all in black leather with a high-collared bloodstained blue cloak thrown back from his shoulders, a sword in one hand and an axe in the other, raising his sword to him from the rail of the doomed galley.

"We're on our way," called Hawkmoon. "Your ship's safe from us . . ."

"Stay a moment!" The black-clad man leapt up and balanced himself on the *River Hawk*'s rail. "I'd like to thank you for doing half our work for us."

Reluctantly Hawkmoon waited until the man had leapt back to his own ship and approached them along the deck.

"I'm Pahl Bewchard and the ship's mine," he said. "I've waited many weeks to catch the *River Hawk* – might not have done so, had you not taken on the best part of the crew and given me time to sneak out of the cove . . ."

"Aye," said Hawkmoon. "Well, I want no further part in a quarrel between pirates . . ."

"You do me a disservice, sir," Bewchard replied easily. "For I'm sworn to rid the river of the Pirate Lords of Starvel. I am their fiercest enemy."

Bewchard's men were swarming back into their own ship, cutting loose the mooring ropes as they came. The *River Hawk* swung round in the current, her stern now below the water-line. Some of the pirates leapt overboard, but there was no sign of Valjon.

"Where did their leader escape to!" D'Averc asked, studying the ship.

"He's like a rat," Bewchard answered. "Doubtless he slipped away as soon as it was plain the day was lost for him. You have helped me greatly, gentlemen, for Valjon is the worst of the pirates. I am grateful."

And D'Averc, never at a loss where courtesy and his own interests were concerned, replied, "And we are grateful to you, Captain Bewchard – for arriving when things seemed lost for us. The debt is settled, it seems." He smiled pleasantly.

Bewchard inclined his head. "Thank you. However, if I may make a somewhat direct statement, you seem in need of something to aid your recovery. Both of you are wounded, your clothes – your clothes are plainly not what you, as gentlemen, would normally choose to wear . . . I mean, in short, that I would be honored if you would accept the hospitality of my ship's galley, such as it is, and the hospitality of my mansion when we dock."

Hawkmoon frowned thoughtfully. He had taken a liking to the young captain. "And where do you plan to dock, sir?"

"In Narleen," replied Bewchard. "Where I live."

"We were, in fact, travelling to Narleen before we were trapped by Valjon," Hawkmoon began.

"Then you must certainly travel with me. If I can be of assistance . . ."

"Thank you, Captain Bewchard," Hawkmoon said. "We should appreciate your aid in reaching Narleen. And perhaps on the way you would be able to supply us with some information which we lack."

"Willingly." Bewchard gestured toward a door set beneath the poop deck. "My cabin is this way, gentlemen."

Chapter Six
NARLEEN

THROUGH THE PORTHOLES of Captain Bewchard's cabin, they saw the spray fly as the ship flung itself downriver under full sail.

"If we should meet a couple of pirates," Bewchard told them, "we should have little chance. That is why we make such speed."

The cook brought in the last of the dishes and laid it before them. There were several kinds of meat, fish and vegetables, fruit and wine. Hawkmoon ate as sparingly as possible, unable to resist at least a sample of everything on the table, but aware that his stomach might not yet be ready for such rich food.

"This is a celebration meal," Bewchard told them cheerfully, "for I have been hunting Valjon for months."

"Who is Valjon?" Hawkmoon asked between munches.

"He seems a strange individual."

"Unlike any pirate I ever imagined," D'Averc put in.

"He is a pirate by tradition," Bewchard told them. "His ancestors have always been pirates, preying on the river traffic for centuries. For a long time the merchants paid huge taxes to the Lords of Starvel, but some years ago they began to resist and Valjon retaliated. Then a group of us decided to build fighting ships, like the pirates', and attack them on the water. I command such a ship. A merchant by trade, I have turned to more military pursuits until Narleen is free of Valjon and his like."

"And how are you faring?" asked Hawkmoon.

"It is hard to say. Valjon and the other Lords are still impregnable in their walled city – Starvel is a city within a city, within Narleen – and so far we have only been able to curb their piracy a little. As yet there has been no major test of strength for either side."

"You say Valjon is a pirate by tradition . . ." D'Averc began.

"Aye, his ancestors came to Narleen many hundreds of years ago. They were powerful and we were relatively weak. Legend says that Valjon's ancestor, Batach Gerandiun, had sorcery to aid him moreover. They built the wall around Starvel, the quarter of the city they took for themselves, and have been there ever since."

"And how does Valjon answer you when you attack his ships as we saw today?" Hawkmoon took a long draft of wine.

"He retaliates with every possible means, but we are beginning to make them warier of venturing onto the river these days. There is still much to do. I would slay Valjon if I could. That would break the power of the whole pirate community, I am sure, but he always escapes. He has an instinct for danger – is always able to avoid it even before it threatens."

"I wish you luck in finding him," Hawkmoon said. "Now tell us, Captain Bewchard, know you anything of a blade called 'The Sword of the Dawn' – we were told that we should find it in Narleen?"

Bewchard looked surprised. "Aye, I've heard of it. It is connected with the legend I told you of – concerning Valjon's ancestor Batach Gerandiun. Batach's sorcerous power was said to be contained in the blade. Batach has become a god since – the pirates have deified him and worship him at their temple which is named after him – the Temple of Batach Gerandiun. They are a superstitious breed, those pirates. Their minds and manners are often unfathomable to the practical merchant kind, like myself."

"And where is the blade now?" D'Averc asked.

"Why, it is said to be the sword that the pirates worship in the temple. It represents their power to them, as well as Batach's. Do you seek to make the blade your own, then, gentlemen?"

"I do not . . ." began Hawkmoon, but D'Averc interrupted smoothly.

"We do, captain. We have a relative – a very wise scholar from the north – who heard of the blade and wished to inspect it. He sent us here to see if it could be bought . . ."

Bewchard laughed heartily. "It could be bought, my friends, it could be – with the blood of half a million fighting men. The pirates would fight to the last man to defend The Sword of the Dawn. It is that which they value above all other things."

Hawkmoon felt his spirits sink. Had the dying Mygan sent them on an impossible quest?

"Ah, well," D'Averc replied, shrugging philosophically. "Then we must hope that you eventually defeat Valjon and the others and put their property up for auction some time."

Bewchard smiled. "I do not think that day will come in my lifetime. It will take many years before Valjon is finally defeated." He rose from his table. "Excuse me for a few moments, I must see how things are on deck."

He left the cabin with a brief, courteous bow.

When he had gone Hawkmoon frowned. "What now, D'Averc? We are stranded in this strange land, unable to get that which we sought." He took Mygan's rings from his pouch and jingled them on the palm of his hand. There were eleven there now, for he and D'Averc had taken their own off. "We are lucky to have these still. Perhaps we should use them – leap at random into the dimensions in the hope of finding a way back to our Kamarg?"

D'Averc snorted. "We might find ourselves suddenly at King Huon's court, or in peril of our lives from some monster. I say we go to Narleen and spend some time there – see just how difficult it will be to obtain the pirate sword." He took something from his own pouch. "Until you spoke I had forgotten that I possessed this little thing." He held it up. It was the

112

charge from one of the guns used in the city of Halapandur.

"And what significance has that, D'Averc?" Hawkmoon asked.

"As I told you, Hawkmoon – it could prove useful to us."

"Without a gun?"

"Without a gun," nodded D'Averc.

As he replaced the charge in his pouch Pahl Bewchard came back through the door. He was smiling.

"Less than an hour, my friends – and we shall be berthing in Narleen," he told them. "I think you will like our city." Then he added with a grin: "At least, that part which is not inhabited by the Pirate Lords."

Hawkmoon and D'Averc stood on the deck of Bewchard's ship and watched as it was skillfully brought into harbor. The sun was hot in a clear, blue sky, making the city shine. The buildings were for the most part quite low, rarely more than four stories, but they were richly decorated with rococo designs that seemed very old. All the colors were muted, weathered, but nonetheless still clear. Much wood was used in the construction of the houses – pillars, balconies and frontages were all of carved wood – but some had painted metal railings and even doors.

The quayside was crowded with crates and bales being loaded or unloaded onto the myriad ships that crowded the harbor. Men worked with derricks to swing them into hatches or onto the quays, hauled them along gangplanks, sweating in the heat of the day, stripped to the waist.

Everywhere was noise and bustle and Bewchard seemed to relish it as he escorted Hawkmoon and D'Averc down the gangplank of his schooner and through the crowd that had begun to gather.

Bewchard was greeted on all sides.

"How did you fare, captain?"

"Did you find Valjon?"

"Have you lost many men?"

At last Bewchard paused, laughing good-humouredly.

"Well, fellow citizens of Narleen," he shouted. "I must tell you, I see, or you shall not let us pass. Aye, we sank Valjon's ship . . ."

There was a gasp from the crowd and then silence. Bewchard

sprang up onto a packing case and raised his arms.

"We sank Valjon's ship, the *River Hawk* – but it would have likely escaped us altogether had it not been for my two companions here."

D'Averc glanced at Hawkmoon in mock embarrassment. The citizens stared at the two in surprise, as if unable to believe that two such ragged starvelings could be anything but lowly slaves.

"These two are your heroes, not I," Bewchard continued. "Singlehanded they resisted the whole pirate crew, killed Ganak, Valjon's lieutenant, and made the ship easy prey to our attack. Then they scuttled the *River Hawk!*"

There was a great cheer now from the crowd.

"Know their names, citizens of Narleen. Remember them as friends of this city and deny them nothing. They are Dorian Hawkmoon of the Black Jewel and Huillam D'Averc. You have not seen braver souls nor finer swordsmen!"

Hawkmoon was genuinely embarrassed by all this and frowned up at Bewchard, trying to signal that he should stop.

"And what of Valjon?" called a member of the crowd. "Is he dead?"

"He escaped us," Bewchard replied regretfully. "He ran like a rat. But we shall have his head one day."

"Or he yours, Bewchard!" The speaker was a richly dressed man who had pushed forward. "All you have done is anger him! For years I paid my river taxes to Valjon's men and they let me ply the river in peace. Now you and your like say 'Pay no taxes' and I do not – but I know no peace these days, cannot sleep without fear of what Valjon will do. Valjon is bound to retaliate. And it might not be only you on whom he takes his vengeance! What of the rest of us – those who want peace of mind and not glory? You endanger us all!"

Bewchard laughed. "It was you, Veroneeg, if I'm not mistaken, who first began to complain about the pirates, said you could not stand the high levies they demanded, supported us when we formed the league to fight Valjon. Well, Veroneeg, we are fighting him, and it is hard, but we shall win, never fear!"

The crowd cheered again, but this time the cheer was a little more ragged and the people were beginning to disperse.

"Valjon will take his vengeance, Bewchard," Veroneeg repeated. "Your days are numbered. There are rumors that the

Pirate Lords are gathering their strength, that they have only been playing with us up to now. They could raze Narleen if they wished!"

"Destroy the source of their livelihood! That would be foolish of them!" Bewchard shrugged as if to dismiss the middle-aged merchant.

"Foolish, perhaps – as foolish as your actions," wheezed Veroneeg. "But make them hate us enough and their hatred might make them forget that it is we who feed them!"

Bewchard smiled and shook his head. "You should retire, Veroneeg. The rigors of merchant life are too much for you."

The crowd had almost completely vanished now and there were looks of anxiety on many of the faces that had only lately been cheering the heroes.

Bewchard jumped down from the box and put his arms around his companions' shoulders. "Come, my friends, let's listen no longer to poor old Veroneeg. He would make any triumph sour with his gloomy prattling. Let's to my mansion and see if we can find you raiment more befitting gentlemen – then, tomorrow, we can go about the city and buy new outfits for you both!"

He led them through the teeming streets of Narleen, streets that wound an apparently logic-less course, that were narrow and smelling of a million mingled odors, that were crowded with sailors and swordsmen and merchants and quay workers, old women, pretty girls, stallkeepers selling their wares and riders picking their way among those on foot. He led them over the cobbles, up a steep hill and out into a square with one side clear of houses. And there was the sea.

Bewchard paused for a moment to stare at the sea. It sparkled in the sunlight.

D'Averc gestured toward it. "You trade beyond that ocean?"

Bewchard unpinned his heavy cloak and threw it over his arm. He opened the collar of his shirt and shook his head, smiling. "Nobody knows what lies beyond the sea – probably nothing. No, we trade along the coast for about two or three hundred miles in each direction. This area is thick with rich cities that did not suffer too badly the effects of the Tragic Millenium."

"I see. And what do you call this continent? Is it, as we suspect, Asiacommunista?"

Bewchard frowned. "I have not heard it called that, though I'm no scholar. I have heard it called variously 'Yarshai', 'Amarehk' and 'Nishtay'." He shrugged. "I am not even sure where it lies in relation to the legendary continents said to lie elsewhere in the world . . ."

"Amarehk!" Hawkmoon exclaimed. "But I had always thought it the legendary home of superhuman creatures . . ."

"And I had thought the Runestaff in Asiacommunista!" D'Averc laughed. "It does not do, friend Hawkmoon, to place too much faith in legends! Perhaps, after all, the Runestaff does not exist!"

Hawkmoon nodded. "Perhaps."

Bewchard was frowning. "The Runestaff – legends – what do you speak of, gentlemen?"

"A point this scholar we mentioned made," D'Averc said hastily. "It would be boring to explain."

Bewchard shrugged. "I hate to be bored, my friends," he said, and led them on through the streets.

They were now beyond the trading part of the city and on a hill in which the houses seemed much richer and less crowded together. High walls surrounded gardens that could be seen to contain flowering trees and fountains.

It was outside the gates of one such walled house that Bewchard at last stopped.

"Welcome to my mansion, my good friends," he said, rapping on the gate.

A covered grille was opened and eyes peered at them. Then the gate was pulled wide and a servant bowed to Bewchard. "Welcome home, master. Was the voyage successful? Your sister awaits you."

"Very successful, Per! Aha – so Jeleana is here to greet us. You will like Jeleana, my friends!"

Chapter Seven
THE BLAZE

JELEANA WAS BEAUTIFUL, a young, raven-haired girl with a vivacious manner that instantly captivated D'Averc. At dinner that night he flirted with her and was delighted when she cheerfully responded.

Bewchard smiled to see them play so wittily, but Hawkmoon found it hard to watch them, for he was reminded painfully of his own Yisselda, his wife who waited for him thousands of miles across the sea and perhaps hundreds of years across time (for he had no way of knowing if the crystal rings had brought him only through space).

Bewchard seemed to detect a melancholy look in Hawkmoon's eye and sought to cheer him up with jokes and anecdotes concerning some of his lighter and more amusing encounters while fighting the pirates of Starvel.

Hawkmoon responded bravely, but he still could not rid his mind of thoughts of his beloved girl, Count Brass's daughter, and how she fared.

Had Taragorm perfected his machines for travelling through time? Had Meliadus found an alternate means of reaching Castle Brass?

The more the evening wore on, the less able Hawkmoon was to continue a light conversation. At length he rose and bowed politely. "I do apologise, Captain Bewchard," he murmured, "but I am very weary. The time spent in the galley – the fighting today . . ."

Jeleana Bewchard and Huillam D'Averc did not notice him rise, for they were engrossed with one another.

Bewchard stood up quickly, a look of concern on his handsome face. "Of course. I apologise, Master Hawkmoon, for my thoughtlessness . . ."

Hawkmoon smiled wanly. "You have not been thoughtless,

117

captain. Your hospitality is magnificent. However . . ."

Bewchard's hand made a movement toward the bell pull, but before he could summon a servant there came a sudden banging on the door. "Enter!" Bewchard commanded.

The servant who had admitted them to the garden earlier that day stood panting in the doorway. "Captain Bewchard! There is a fire at the quayside – a ship is burning."

"A ship? Which ship?"

"Your ship, captain – the one you came home in today!"

Instantly Bewchard was making for the door, Hawkmoon and D'Averc following rapidly behind him, Jeleana behind them.

"A carriage, Per," he ordered. "Hurry, man! A carriage!"

Within moments an enclosed carriage drawn by four horses was brought round to the front of the house and Bewchard climbed in, waiting impatiently for Hawkmoon and D'Averc to join him. Jeleana tried to enter the carriage, but he shook his head. "No, Jeleana. We do not know what is happening on the quays. Wait here!"

Then the carriage was off, bumping over the cobbles at an alarming rate, making for the dockside.

The narrow streets were lit with torches stuck in brackets attached to the sides of houses and the carriage flung a black shadow on the walls as it passed, bumping and crashing through the streets.

At last the quayside was reached, illuminated by more than torches, for in the harbor a schooner blazed. Everywhere was confusion as masters of vessels arrived to bully their men aboard their own craft and move them away from Bewchard's schooner, for fear that they, too, would be set afire.

Bewchard leapt from the carriage, closely followed by Hawkmoon and D'Averc. He ran for the quayside, elbowing his way through the crowd, but once by the water he paused and hung his head.

"It's hopeless," he murmured in despair. "She's gone. This could only have been Valjon's work . . ."

Veroneeg, his face sweating and red in the glare from the burning ship, burst from the crowd. "You see, Bewchard – Valjon is taking his vengeance! I warned you!"

They turned at the sound of galloping hooves, saw a rider rein in his horse close by. "Bewchard!" the man cried. "Pahl

Bewchard who claims to have sunk the *River Hawk!*"

Bewchard looked up. "I am Bewchard. Who are you?"

The rider was clad in bizarre finery and in his left hand he clutched a scroll which he brandished. "I am Valjon's man – his messenger!" He threw the scroll toward Bewchard who let it lie where it had fallen.

"What is it?" Bewchard said between gritted teeth.

"It is a bill, Bewchard. A bill for fifty men and forty slaves, for a ship and all furnishings, plus twenty-five thousand smaygars' worth of treasure. Valjon, too, can play the merchant game!"

Bewchard glared at the messenger. The light from the blazing ship sent shadows flickering across his face. He spurned the scroll with his foot, kicking it into the debris-filled water.

"You seek to frighten me with this melodrama, I see!" he said firmly. "Well, tell Valjon I do not intend to pay his bill and that I am not frightened. Tell him – if he wishes to 'play the merchant game' – that he and his greedy ancestors owe the people of Narleen considerably more than the amount on his bill. I will continue to reclaim that debt."

The rider opened his mouth as if to speak, then changed his mind, spat on the cobbles and wheeled his horse about, galloping away into the darkness.

"He will kill you now, Bewchard," said Veroneeg almost triumphantly. "He will kill you now. I hope he realises that not all of us are as foolish as you!"

"And I hope that we are not all as foolish as you, Veroneeg," answered Bewchard contemptuously. "If Valjon is threatening me, it means that I have succeeded – partially at least – in unnerving him!"

He stalked toward his carriage and stood aside while Hawkmoon and D'Averc climbed in. Then he entered, slammed the door and tapped with the hilt of his sword on the roof, signalling the driver to return to the mansion.

"Are you sure that Valjon is as weak as you suggest?" Hawkmoon asked hesitantly.

Bewchard smiled at him grimly.

"I am sure that he is stronger than I suggest – stronger perhaps than Veroneeg thinks. My own opinion is that Valjon is still somewhat surprised that we have had the temerity to attack his ship as we did today, that he has not yet marshalled all his resources. But it would not do to tell Veroneeg that, would it, my friend?"

Hawkmoon looked at Bewchard admiringly. "You have much courage, captain."

"Desperation, possibly, friend Hawkmoon."

Hawkmoon nodded. "I know what you mean I think."

The rest of the return journey was made in thoughtful silence.

At the mansion the garden gate was open and they drove straight into the drive. At the main door to the house Jeleana awaited them pale-faced.

"Are you unharmed, Pahl?" she asked as he descended from the carriage.

"Of course," replied Bewchard. "You seem unduly frightened, Jeleana."

She turned and walked back into the house, back into the dining room where their supper still lay on the table.

"It – it was not the burning ship that made me thus," she told him trembling. She looked at her brother, then at D'Averc, lastly at Hawkmoon. Her eyes were wide. "We had a visitor while you were gone."

"A visitor? Who was it?" Bewchard asked, putting his arm around her shaking shoulders.

"He – he came alone . . ." she began.

"And what is so remarkable about a visitor coming alone? Where is he now?"

"It was Valjon, Pahl – Lord Valjon of Starvel himself. He . . ." she put her hand to her face. "He stroked my face – he looked at me from those bleak, inhuman eyes of his, he spoke in that voice . . ."

"And what did he say?" Hawkmoon asked suddenly, his tone grim. "What did he say, Lady Jeleana?"

Again her eyes went from one to the other, to return to Hawkmoon.

"He said that he is merely playing with Pahl, that he is too proud to spend all his time and strength in pursuing a vendetta against him, that unless Pahl proclaims in the city square tomorrow that he will cease bothering the Pirate Lords with his – his 'silly' harrying of them – Pahl will be punished in a way that will be suitable to his particular misdemeanor. He said that he expects to hear that the proclamation has been made by midday tomorrow."

Bewchard frowned. "He came here, to my own house, to display his contempt for me, I suppose. The burning of the ship was just a demonstration – and a diversion to get me to the quayside. He spoke to you, Jeleana, to show that he can reach my nearest and most beloved whenever he chooses." Bewchard sighed. "There is no question now that he not only threatens my life, but the lives of those close to me. It is a trick that I should have expected – did half-expect, yet . . ."

He looked up at Hawkmoon, his eyes suddenly tired.

"Perhaps I have been a fool, after all, Master Hawkmoon. Perhaps Veroneeg was right. I cannot fight Valjon – not while he fights from the security of Starvel. I have no weapons such as those he employs against me!"

"I cannot advise you," said Hawkmoon quietly. "But I can offer you my services – and D'Averc's here – in your struggle, should you wish to continue it."

Bewchard looked directly into Hawkmoon's face then and he laughed, straightening his shoulders.

"You do not advise me, Dorian Hawkmoon of the Black Jewel, but you do indicate to me what I should think of myself if I refused the aid of two such swordsmen as yourself. Aye – I'll fight on. Indeed, tomorrow I shall spend relaxing, ignoring Valjon's warning. You, Jeleana, I will have guarded here. I will send for father and ask him to bring his guards to protect you both. Hawkmoon, D'Averc and myself – why – we'll shop tomorrow." He indicated the borrowed clothes that the two men wore. "I promised you new suits – and a good sheath, I think, Master Hawkmoon, for your borrowed sword – Valjon's sword. We will be casual tomorrow. We will show Valjon – and, more important, the people of this city – that we are not frightened by Valjon's threats."

D'Averc nodded soberly. "It is the only way, I think, if the spirit of your fellow citizens is not to be destroyed," he said. "Then, even if you die, you die a hero – and inspire those who follow you."

"I hope I do not die," Bewchard smiled, "for I have a great love for life. Still, we shall see, my friends. We shall see."

Chapter Eight
THE WALLS OF STARVEL

NEXT DAY DAWNED as hot as the previous day and Pahl Bewchard sauntered out with his friends.

As they moved through the streets of Narleen, it was plain that many already knew of Valjon's ultimatum and were wondering what Bewchard would do.

Bewchard did nothing. Nothing but smile at all he met, kiss the hands of a few ladies, greet a couple of acquaintances, leading Hawkmoon and D'Averc toward the center of the town where he had recommended a good outfitter.

That the outfitter's shop was barely a stone's throw from the walls of Starvel suited Bewchard's purpose.

"After midday," he said, "we shall visit the outfitter's. But before then we will take lunch at a tavern I can vouch for. It lies close to the central square and many of our leading citizens drink there. We shall be seen to be relaxed and untroubled. We will talk of small things and not mention Valjon's threats at all, no matter how many efforts are made to bring the subject up."

"You are asking a great deal, Captain Bewchard," D'Averc pointed out.

"Perhaps," Bewchard answered, "but I have a feeling that much hangs on this day's events – more than I understand at this moment. I am gambling on those events – for it could be that the day could mean victory or defeat for me."

Hawkmoon nodded but made no comment. He too, sensed something in the air and could not question Bewchard's instinct.

The tavern was visited, food eaten, wine drunk, and they pretended not to notice that they were the center of attention, cleverly avoiding all attempts to quiz them on what they intended to do about Valjon's ultimatum.

The hour of noon came and went and Bewchard sat and

chatted with his friends for a further hour before rising, putting down his wine cup and saying, "Now, gentlemen, this outfitter I mentioned . . ."

The streets were unusually lacking in crowds as they walked casually through them, getting closer and closer to the center of the city. But there were many curtains that moved as they passed, many faces seen at windows, and Bewchard grinned, as if relishing the situation.

"We are the only actors on the stage today, my friends," he said. "We must play our parts well."

Then at last Hawkmoon saw his first glimpse of the walls of Starvel. They rose above the rooftops, white and proud and enigmatic, seemingly without gates.

"There are a few small gates," Bewchard told Hawkmoon, "but they are rarely used. Instead they have huge underground waterways and docks. These, of course, lead directly to the river."

Bewchard led them into a sidestreet and indicated a sign about halfway down. "There, my friends – there's our outfitter."

They entered the shop crammed with bales of cloth, with heaps of cloaks and jerkins and britches, swords and daggers of all description, fine harness, helmets, hats, boots, belts and everything else that a man could possibly want to wear. The owner of the shop was serving another customer as they entered. The owner was a middle-aged man, well-built and genial, with a red face and pure white hair. He smiled at Bewchard and the customer turned – a youth whose eyes widened when he saw the three standing in the doorway of the shop. The youth muttered something and made to leave.

"You do not want the sword, master?" the outfitter asked in surprise. "I would drop my price by half a smaygar, but not more."

"Another time, Pyahr, another time," answered the youth hurriedly, bowed swiftly to Bewchard and left the shop.

"Who was that?" asked Hawkmoon with a smile.

"Veroneeg's son, if I remember right," Bewchard replied. He laughed. "He has inherited his father's cowardice!"

Pyahr came up. "Good afternoon, Captain Bewchard. I had not expected to see you here today. You did not make the announcement expected of you?"

"No, Pyahr, I did not."

Pyahr smiled. "I had a feeling you wouldn't, captain. However, you are in considerable danger now. Valjon will have to pursue the matter, will he not?"

"He will have to try, Pyahr."

"He will try soon, captain. He will waste no time. Are you sure it is wise to come so close to the walls of Starvel?"

"I have to show that I am not afraid of Valjon," Bewchard answered. "Besides, why should I change my plans for him? I promised my friends here that they could choose clothing from the finest outfitter in Narleen and I am not a man to forget a promise like that!"

Pyahr smiled and made a dismissive gesture with his hand. "I wish you luck, captain. Now, gentleman, what do you see that you like?"

Hawkmoon picked up a cloak of rich scarlet, fingering its golden clasp. "I see much that I like. You have a fine shop, Master Pyahr."

While Bewchard chatted with the shopkeeper, Hawkmoon and D'Averc wandered slowly around the shop, picking out a shirt here and a pair of boots there. Two hours passed before they had finally made up their minds.

"Why do you not go into my dressing rooms and try on the clothes?" Pyahr suggested. "I think you have chosen well, gentlemen."

Hawkmoon and D'Averc retired into the dressing rooms. Hawkmoon had a shirt of silk in a deep lavender shade, a jerkin of soft, light-colored brushed leather, a scarf of purple and fine, flaring britches that were also of silk and a purple that matched the scarf, which he knotted about his neck. These britches he tucked into boots of the same leather as the jerkin, which he left unbuttoned. He drew a wide leather belt about his waist and then clasped a cloak of deep blue over his shoulders.

D'Averc had taken for himself a scarlet shirt and matching britches, a jerkin of shining black leather and boots that were also of black leather and reached almost to his knees. Over this he drew a cloak of stiff silk, colored deep purple. He was reaching for his sword belt when there came a shout from the shop.

Hawkmoon parted the curtains of the dressing room.

The shop was suddenly full of men – evidently pirates from Starvel. They had surrounded Bewchard who had not had time to draw his sword.

Hawkmoon wheeled and picked up his sword from the pile of discarded clothing, rushing into the shop to collide with Pyahr who was staggering back, blood pumping from his throat.

Even now the pirates were backing out of the shop and Bewchard could not even be seen.

Hawkmoon stabbed a pirate directly in the heart, defended himself from another's thrust.

"Do not try to fight us," snarled the pirate who had tried to stab him, "we want only Bewchard!"

"Then you must kill us before you take him," cried D'Averc who had joined Hawkmoon.

"Bewchard goes to find his punishment for insulting our Lord Valjon," the pirate told him and slashed at him.

D'Averc leapt back bringing his sword up in a flickering movement that knocked the pirate's blade from his hand. The man snarled, hurling the dagger that was in his other hand, but D'Averc deflected this, also, thrusting out to take the man in the throat.

Now half the pirates had detached themselves from their fellows and advanced on Hawkmoon and D'Averc who were pressed backward into the shop.

"They're escaping with Bewchard," Hawkmoon said desperately. "We must aid him."

He thrust savagely at his attackers, trying to cut his way through them to go to Bewchard's assistance, but then he heard D'Averc yell from behind him.

"More of them – coming through the back exit!"

That was the last he heard before he felt a sword hilt slam against the base of his skull and he fell forward onto a heap of shirts.

He awoke feeling smothered and rolled over onto his back. It was getting dark inside the shop and it was strangely silent now.

He staggered up, his sword still in his hand. The first thing he saw was Pyahr's corpse sprawled near the curtains of the dressing room.

The second thing he saw was what seemed to be D'Averc's corpse lying stretched across the bale of orange cloth, blood covering most of his features.

Hawkmoon went to his friend, put his hand inside his jerkin

125

and with relief heard his heart beating. Like him, it seemed, D'Averc had only been stunned. Doubtless the pirates had left them behind intentionally, wanting someone to tell the citizens of Narleen what befell those who, like Pahl Bewchard, offended the Lord Valjon.

Hawkmoon stumbled to the back of the shop and found a pitcher of water. He carried it back to where his friend lay and put the pitcher to D'Averc's lips, then he tore off a strip from the bale of cloth and bathed the face. The blood had come from a broad but shallow cut across the temple.

D'Averc began to stir, opened his eyes and looked directly into Hawkmoon's.

"Bewchard," he said. "We must rescue him, Hawkmoon."

Hawkmoon nodded bleakly. "Aye. But he is in Starvel by now."

"No one knows that but us," D'Averc said rising stiffly to a sitting position. "If we could rescue him and bring him back, then tell the city the story, think what that would do for the citizens' morale."

"Very well," said Hawkmoon. "We shall pay a visit to Starvel – and pray that Bewchard still lives." He sheathed his sword. "We must climb those walls somehow, D'Averc. We shall need equipment."

"Doubtless we'll find all we need in this shop," D'Averc replied. "Come, let us move swiftly. It is already nightfall."

Hawkmoon fingered the black jewel set in his forehead. His thoughts went again to Yisselda, to Count Brass, Oladahn and Bowgentle, wondering about their fate, His whole impulse was to forget about Bewchard, forget about Mygan's instructions, the legendary Sword of the Dawn and the equally legendary Runestaff, to steal one of the ships from the harbor and set off across the sea to try to find his beloved. But then he sighed and straightened his back. They could not leave Bewchard to his fate. They must try to rescue him or die.

He thought of the walls of Starvel that lay so close. Perhaps no one had tried to scale them before, for they were very steep and doubtless well-guarded. Perhaps it could be done, however. They would have to try.

Chapter Nine
THE TEMPLE OF BATACH GERANDIUN

EACH WITH MORE than a score of daggers stuck in their belts, Hawkmoon and D'Averc began to scale the walls of Starvel.

Hawkmoon went first, wrapping cloth around the hilt of a dagger and then searching for a crack in the stone into which to insert the point of the dagger and then tap it gently into place, praying that no one above would hear him and that the dagger would hold.

Slowly they ascended the wall, testing the daggers as they went. Once Hawkmoon felt a blade begin to give beneath his foot, clung to the dagger he had just inserted above his head – and then felt that begin to work loose, too. A hundred feet below was the street. Desperately he took another dagger from his belt and hunted for a crack in the stone, found one and plunged the blade in. It held, while the dagger supporting his foot fell away. He heard a thin clatter as it landed in the street. Now he hung, unable to move up or down, as D'Averc tried to insert another dagger into the crack. At last he succeeded and Hawkmoon breathed with relief. They were near the top of the wall now. Only a few more feet to go – and no idea what awaited either on the wall or beyond it.

Perhaps their efforts were useless? Perhaps Bewchard was already dead? There was no point in thinking such thoughts now.

Hawkmoon went even more cautiously as he reached the top. He heard a footfall above him and knew that a guard was passing. He paused in his work. Only one more dagger and he would be able to gain the top of the wall. He glanced down, saw D'Averc's face grim in the moonlight. The footfalls died away and he continued tapping in the dagger.

Then, just as he was heaving himself upwards the footsteps

came back, moving much more rapidly than before. Hawkmoon looked up – directly into the face of a startled pirate.

Instantly Hawkmoon risked everything, sprang for the top of the wall, grasped it as the man drew his blade, flung himself upwards and struck with all his might at the man's legs.

The pirate gasped, tried to regain his balance, and then fell soundlessly.

Breathing rapidly, Hawkmoon reached down and helped D'Averc to the top of the wall. Running along it now came two more guards.

Hawkmoon rose, drew his sword and prepared to meet them.

Metal clashed on metal as D'Averc and Hawkmoon engaged the two pirates. The exchange was short, for the two companions had little time to waste and were desperate. Almost as one their blades struck for the hearts of the pirate guards, sank into flesh and were withdrawn. Almost as one the guards collapsed and lay still.

Hawkmoon and D'Averc glanced up and down the length of the wall. It seemed that they had not yet been detected by others. Hawkmoon pointed to a stairway leading down to the ground. D'Averc nodded and they made their way toward it, descending softly and as rapidly as they dared, hoping no one would come up.

It was dark and quiet below. It seemed a city of the dead. Far away, in the center of Starvel, a beacon gleamed, but—elsewhere all was in darkness, save for a little light that escaped from the shutters of windows or through the cracks in doors.

As they drew nearer to the ground they heard a few sounds from the houses – the sounds of coarse laughter and of roistering. Once a door opened showing a crowded, drunken scene inside, and a pirate staggered drunkenly out cursing something, falling flat on his face on the cobbles. The door closed, the pirate did not stir.

The buildings of Starvel were simpler than those beyond the wall. They did not have the rich decoration of Narleen and, if Hawkmoon had not known better, he would have thought that Starvel was the poorer city. But Bewchard had told him that the pirates only displayed their wealth on their ships, their backs and in the mysterious Temple of Batach Gerandiun where the Sword of the Dawn was said to hang.

They crept into the streets, swords ready. Even assuming

Bewchard was still alive, they had no idea where he was being held prisoner, but something drew them towards the beacon in the center of the city.

Then, when they were quite close to the light, the sonorous boom of a drum suddenly filled the air, echoing through the dark, empty streets. Then they heard the tramp of feet, the clatter of horses' hooves nearby.

"What's that?" hissed D'Averc. He peered cautiously around a building and then rapidly withdrew his head. "They're coming towards us," he said. "Get back!"

Torchlight began to flicker and huge shadows swam into the street ahead of them. Hawkmoon and D'Averc backed away into the darkness, watching as a procession began to file past.

It was led by Valjon himself, his pale face stark and rigid, his eyes staring straight ahead of him as he rode a black horse through the streets towards the place where the beacon burned. Behind him were drummers, beating out a slow, monotonous rhythm, and behind them another group of armed horsemen, all richly clad and plainly the other Lords of Starvel. Their faces, too, were set and they sat in their saddles as stiffly as statues. But it was that which came behind these pirate lords that chiefly caught the watchers' attention.

It was Bewchard.

His arms and legs were stretched out on a great frame of bent whalebone that was fixed upright upon a wheeled platform drawn by six horses led by liveried pirates. He was pale and his naked body was covered in sweat. He was evidently in great pain, but his lips were pressed grimly together. On his torso strange symbols had been painted and there were similar markings on his cheeks. His muscles strained as he struggled to free himself from the cords biting into his ankles and wrists, but he was securely bound.

D'Averc made a movement to spring forward, but Hawkmoon restrained him.

"No," he whispered. "Follow them. We might have a better chance to save him later."

They let the rest of the procession pass and then crept after it. It moved slowly on until it entered a wide square that was lit by the great beacon glowing over the doorway of a tall building of strange, assymetrical architecture that seemed almost to have been formed naturally out of some glassy, volcanic stuff. It was an ominous construction.

"The Temple of Batach Gerandiun without question," Hawkmoon murmured. "I wonder why they take him there?"

"Let us find out," D'Averc said as the procession filed into the temple.

Together, they darted across the square and crouched in the shadows near the door. It was half-open and apparently no attempt had been made to guard it. Perhaps the pirates believed that no one would dare enter such a place unless it was their right.

Looking about him to see if they were observed, Hawkmoon crept toward the door and pushed it slowly open. He was in a dark passage. From round a corner came a reddish glow and the sound of chanting. D'Averc close behind him, Hawkmoon began to move down the corridor.

Hawkmoon paused before he reached the corner. A strange smell was in his nostrils, a disgusting smell that was at once familiar and unfamiliar. He shuddered and took a step back. D'Averc's face wrinkled in nausea. "Ugh – what is it?"

Hawkmoon shook his head. "Something about it – the smell of blood, perhaps. Yet not just blood . . ."

D'Averc's eyes were wide as he looked at Hawkmoon. It seemed that he was about to suggest that they go no further, but then he squared his shoulders and took a stronger grip on his sword. He took off the scarf he wore around his throat and pressed it to his nose and lips in an ostentatious gesture which reminded Hawkmoon much more of D'Averc's normal self and made him grin, but he followed D'Averc's action and unwound his own scarf and placed it to his face.

Then they moved forward again, turning the corner of the passage.

The light grew brighter, a rosy radiance not unlike the color of fresh blood. It emanated from a doorway at the far end of the corridor, seeming to pulse to the rhythm of the chanting which now grew louder and held a note of terrible menace. The stench, too, grew worse as they advanced.

Once a figure crossed the space from which the pulsing radiance poured. Hawkmoon and D'Averc stood stock still but were unseen. The silhouette vanished and they continued to advance.

Just as the stench assailed their nostrils, so the chanting

began to offend their ears. There was something weirdly off-key about it, something that grated on their nerves. With their eyes half-blinded by the rosy light, it seemed that all their senses were under attack at once. But still they pressed on until they stood only a foot or two from the entrance.

They stared at a scene that made them shudder.

The hall was roughly circular, but with a roof whose height varied enormously, sometimes a few feet above the ground, sometimes disappearing into the smoky darkness. In this it resembled the outward appearance of the building, seeming to be less artificial than organic, rising and falling in a purely arbitrary way as far as Hawkmoon could tell. All the glassy walls reflected the rosy radiance so that the whole scene was stained red.

The light came from a place high in the roof and it drew Hawkmoon's wincing gaze upward.

He recognised it immediately, recognised the thing hanging there, dominating the hall. It was without doubt the thing that Mygan had sent him, with his dying breath, here to find.

"The Sword of the Dawn," whispered D'Averc. "The foul thing can have no part in our destinies, surely!"

Hawkmoon's face was grim. He shrugged. "That is not now what we are here to take. He is what we have come for . . ." and he pointed.

Below the sword were stretched a dozen figures, all on the whalebone frames, arranged in a semi-circle. Not all the men and women on the frames were alive, but most were dying.

D'Averc turned his face away from the sight but then, his expression one of purest horror, forced himself to look back again.

"By the Runestaff!" he gasped. "It's – it's barbaric."

Veins had been cut in the naked bodies and from those veins the lifeblood pumped slowly.

The wretches on the bone frames were being bled to death. Those who lived had faces twisted in anguish and their struggles weakened gradually as their blood dripped, dripped into the pit below them, a pit that had been carved from the obsidian rock.

It was a pit, too, in which things moved, rising to the surface to lap at the fresh blood as it fell, then darting down again. Dark shapes moving in the deep pool of blood.

How deep was the pool? How many thousands had died to fill it? What peculiar properties did the pool contain so that the blood did not congeal?

Around the pool were clustered the Pirate Lords of Starvel, chanting and swaying, their faces lifted up to the Sword of the Dawn. Immediately below the sword, his body straining on the frame, Bewchard hung.

There was a knife in Valjon's hand and there was no doubting the use he intended to make of it. Bewchard stared down at him with loathing and said something that Hawkmoon could not hear. The knife glistened as if already wet with blood, the chanting grew louder and Valjon's hollow tones could be heard through it.

"Sword of the Dawn, in which the spirit of our god and ancestor dwells, Sword of the Dawn, which made Batach Gerandiun invincible and won us all we have, Sword of the Dawn, which makes the dead come alive, causes the living to remain living, which draws its light from the lifeblood of Men, Sword of the Dawn accept this, our latest sacrifice, and continue to know that you shall be worshipped for all time for while you stay in the Temple of Batach Gerandiun, then Starvel shall never fall! Take this thing, this enemy of ours, this upstart, take this Pahl Bewchard of that coarse caste who call themselves merchants!"

Bewchard spoke again, his lips writhing, but his voice could not be heard above the hysterical chanting of the other Pirate Lords.

The knife began to move toward Bewchard's body and Hawkmoon could not restrain himself. The battlecry of his ancestors came automatically to his lips and he screamed the wild bird-cry and voiced the words:

"Hawkmoon! Hawkmoon!"

And he dashed forward at the gathered ghouls, at the noisome pit and its terrible denizens, the frames on which the dead and dying were stretched, the shining, awesome sword.

"Hawkmoon! Hawkmoon!"

The Pirate Lords turned, their chanting over. Valjon's eyes widened in rage and he cast back his robe to reveal a sword that was the twin to the one Hawkmoon carried. He cast the knife into the pit of blood and drew his blade.

"Fool! Know you not that it is a truth that no stranger who

132

enters Batach's temple ever leaves until his body is drained of its blood?"

"It is your body that will bleed tonight, Valjon!" cried Hawkmoon, and he struck at his enemy. But suddenly there were twenty men blocking his way to Valjon, twenty blades against his one.

He lashed at them in fury, his throat clogged with the dreadful stench, his eyes dazzled by the light from the sword, catching glimpses of Bewchard struggling in his bonds. He stabbed and a man died, he slashed and another staggered back into the pit to be dragged down by whatever dwelt there, he hacked and another pirate lost a hand. D'Averc, too, did well and they held the pirates at bay.

For a while it seemed their fury would carry them through all the pirates to Bewchard and save him. Hawkmoon hacked his way into the group and managed to reach the edge of the terrible bloodfilled pit, tried to cut Bewchard's bonds while he fought off the pirates at the same time. But then his foot slipped on the edge of the pool and he sank into it up to his ankle. He felt something touch his foot, something sinuous and disgusting, withdrew as fast as he could and found his arms clutched by pirates.

He flung back his head and called: "I am sorry, Bewchard – I was impetuous – but there was no time, no time!"

"You should not have followed me!" Bewchard cried in misery. "Now you, too, shall suffer my fate and feed the monsters of the pit! You should not have followed me, Hawkmoon!"

Chapter Ten
A FRIEND FROM THE SHADOWS

"I AM AFRAID, friend Bewchard, that your generosity was wasted on us!"

Even in this predicament D'Averc could not resist the irony.

He and Hawkmoon were spreadeagled on either side of Bewchard. Two of the dead sacrificial victims had been cut down and they had replaced them. Below the black things rose and dived restlessly in the pool of blood. Above the light from the Sword of the Dawn cast a red glow throughout the hall, cast a glow upon the upturned, expectant faces of the Pirate Lords, upon Valjon's face as his brooding eyes stared with a kind of triumph at their stripped bodies which, like Bewchard's, had been daubed with peculiar symbols.

There were strange plopping noises below as the creatures in the pit swam about in the blood, waiting, no doubt, for the fresh blood to fall into their pool. Hawkmoon shuddered and barely restrained himself from vomiting. His head ached and his limbs felt weak and incredibly painful. He thought of Yisselda, of his home and his efforts to wage war on the Dark Empire. Now he would never see his wife again, never breathe the air of the Kamarg, never aid in the downfall of Granbretan, should that time ever come. And he had lost all that in a vain effort to save a stranger, a man he hardly knew, whose fight was remote and unimportant compared with the fight against the Dark Empire.

Now it was too late to consider those things, for he was going to die. He would die in a terrible way, bled like a pig, feeling his strength ebbing from him with every pulse of his heart.

Valjon smiled.

"You do not call out a bold battle-cry now, my slave friend. You seem silent. Have you nothing to ask me? Would you not beg for your life – beg to be made my slave again? Would you not apologise for sinking my ship, for killing my men, for insulting me?"

Hawkmoon spat at him but missed.

Valjon gave a slight shrug. "I wait for a new knife. When that is brought and properly blessed, then I shall slit your veins here and there, making sure that you die very slowly, that you will be able to see your blood feeding the ones below. Your bloodless corpses will be sent to the Mayor of Narleen – Bewchard's uncle if I'm not mistaken – as evidence that we of Starvel do not expect to be disobeyed."

A pirate came through the hall and kneeled at Valjon's feet, offering him a long, sharp knife. Valjon accepted it and the pirate backed away.

Valjon now murmured words over the knife, looking often up at the Sword of the Dawn, then he took the knife in his right hand and raised it until its tip was almost touching Hawkmoon's groin.

"Now we shall begin again," said Valjon, and slowly he began to chant the litany that Hawkmoon had heard earlier.

Hawkmoon tasted bile in his mouth as he tried to break free of the cords that bound him. The words droned on, the chanting rose in volume and in pitch of hysteria.

". . . Sword of the Dawn, which makes the dead come alive, causes the living to remain living . . ."

The tip of the knife stroked Hawkmoon's thigh.

". . . which draws its light from the lifeblood of Men . . ."

Absently, Hawkmoon wondered if, indeed, the rosy sword did derive its light, in some peculiar way, from blood. The knife touched his knee and he shuddered again, cursing at Valjon, struggling wildly in the bonds.

". . . know that you shall be worshipped for all time . . ."

Suddenly Valjon paused in his chanting and gasped, looking beyond Hawkmoon to a spot above his head. Hawkmoon craned his neck back and gasped, too.

The Sword of the Dawn was descending from the roof!

It came slowly and then Hawkmoon could see that it hung in a kind of web of metallic ropes – and there was something else in the web, now – the figure of a man.

The man wore a long helmet that hid all his face. His armor and trappings were all black and golden and at his side he bore a huge broadsword.

Hawkmoon could not believe it. He recognised the man – if man it was.

"The Warrior in Jet and Gold!" he cried.

"At your service," said a sardonic voice from within the helm.

Valjon snarled with rage and flung the knife at the Warrior in Jet and Gold. It clattered on his armor and fell into the pool.

The Warrior hung by one gauntleted hand to the pommel of the Sword of the Dawn and carefully cut at the thongs holding Hawkmoon's wrists.

"You – you desecrate our most holy object," Valjon said unbelievingly. "Why are you not punished? Our god, Batach Gerandiun, will have his vengeance. The sword is his, it contains his spirit."

"I know better," said the Warrior. "The sword is Hawk-moon's. The Runestaff saw fit, once, to use your ancestor Batach Gerandiun for its purposes, giving him power over this rosy blade, but now you have lost the power and Hawkmoon here has it!"

"I do not understand you?" Valjon said baffled. "And who are you? Where do you come from? Are you – could you be – Batach Gerandiun?"

"I could be," murmured the Warrior. "I could be many things, many men."

Hawkmoon prayed that the Warrior would be finished in time. Valjon would not remain so dazed forever. He clung to the frame as his wrists came free, took the knife the Warrior handed him, began gingerly to cut at the thongs binding his ankles.

Valjon shook his head.

"This is impossible. A nightmare." He turned to his fellow pirates. "Do you see it, too – the man who hangs from our sword?"

They nodded dumbly, then one of them began to run back towards the entrance of the hall. "I'll fetch men. Men to aid us . . ."

Hawkmoon sprang then – sprang for the nearest pirate lord and grasped him by the throat. The man cried out, tried to wrench Hawkmoon's hands away, but Hawkmoon bent back his head until the neck snapped, swiftly drew the sword from the corpse's scabbard and let the body drop.

There he stood, naked in the glow from the great sword, while the Warrior in Jet and Gold cut at the bonds of his friends.

Valjon backed away, his eyes disbelieving. "It cannot be. It cannot be . . ."

Now D'Averc swung down to stand beside Hawkmoon, then Bewchard joined him. Both were unarmed and naked.

Nonplussed by their leader's indecision, the other pirates made no move. Behind the naked trio, the Warrior in Jet and Gold swung on the great sword, dragging it nearer to the floor.

Valjon screamed and grabbed for the blade, wrenching it from its web of metal. "It is mine! It is mine by right!"

The Warrior in Jet and Gold shook his head. "It is Hawk-moon's – Hawkmoon's by right!"

Valjon clutched the sword to him. "He shall not have it! Destroy them!"

Now men were rushing into the hall, bearing brands, and the pirate lords drew their swords, began to advance on the four who stood by the pool. The Warrior in Jet and Gold drew his own great blade and swept it before him like a scythe, driving the pirates back, killing several.

"Take up their swords," he told Bewchard and D'Averc. "Now we must fight."

Bewchard and D'Averc did as the Warrior instructed and, following behind him, pushed forward.

But now it seemed that a thousand men filled the hall, all with gleaming eyes that lusted for their lives.

"You must take that sword from Valjon, Hawkmoon," shouted the Warrior above the din of battle. "Take it – or we shall all perish!"

Again they were pressed back to the edge of the bloody pit and behind them there came a slobbering sound. Hawkmoon darted a look into the pit and cried out in horror. "They are rising from the pool!"

And now the creatures swam toward the edge and Hawkmoon saw that they were like the tentacled creature they had encountered in the forest, but smaller. Evidently they were of the same breed, brought here centuries before by Valjon's ancestors, gradually adapting from an environment of water to an environment of human blood!

He felt a tentacle touch his naked flesh and he shuddered in cold terror. The peril at his back gave him extra strength and he drove with all his might at the pirates, seeking out Valjon who stood nearby, clutching at the Sword of the Dawn which engulfed him in its weird, red radiance.

Seeing his danger, Valjon moved his hand to the hilt of the sword, called out something and waited expectantly. But what he expected to happen did not and he gasped, running at Hawkmoon with the sword raised high.

Hawkmoon sidestepped, blocked the blow and staggered, half-blinded by the light. Valjon screamed and swung the rosy sword again. Hawkmoon ducked beneath the swing and brought his own blade in, catching Valjon in the shoulder. With a great, bewildered cry Valjon struck again and again his blow was avoided by the naked man.

Valjon paused, studying Hawkmoon's face, his expression one of mingled terror and astonishment. "How can it be?" he murmured. "How can it be?"

Hawkmoon laughed then. "Do not ask me, Valjon, for all this is as much a mystery to me as it is to you. But I was told to take your sword, and take it I shall!" And with that he aimed another thrust at Valjon which the Pirate Lord deflected with a sweeping motion of the Sword of the Dawn.

Now it was Valjon's back that was toward the pit and Hawkmoon saw that the things, blood streaming down their scaly sides, were beginning to crawl onto the floor. Hawkmoon drove the Pirate Lord back, further and further toward the dreadful creatures. He saw a tentacle reach out and catch Valjon's leg, heard the man scream in fear and try to hack at the tentacle with his blade.

Hawkmoon stepped forward then, aimed a blow at Valjon's face with his fist and, with his other hand, wrenched the sword from the Pirate Lord's hand.

Then he watched grimly as Valjon was dragged slowly into the pool.

Valjon stretched out his hands to Hawkmoon. "Save me – please save me, Hawkmoon."

But Hawkmoon's eyes were bleak and he did nothing, simply stood with his hands on the pommel of the Sword of the Dawn as Valjon was dragged closer and closer to the pit of blood.

Valjon said nothing further but covered his face with his hands as first one leg and then the other was drawn into the pool.

There was a long, despairing scream then, that ended in a gurgle of terror, and Valjon disappeared beneath the surface of the pool.

Hawkmoon turned now, hefting the heavy sword and marvelling at the light which shone from it. He took it in both hands and looked to see how his friends were faring. They stood in a tight group, fighting off scores of enemies and it was plain that they would have been overwhelmed by now had it not been for the fact that the pool was disgorging its terrible contents.

The Warrior saw that he had the blade now and cried out something, but Hawkmoon could not hear it. He was forced to bring the sword up to defend himself as a knot of pirates came at him, drove them back and cut through them in an effort to join his friends.

The things from the pit were crowding the edge now, slithering over the floor, and Hawkmoon realised that their position was virtually hopeless, for they were trapped between a horde of swordsmen on one hand and the creatures of the pool on the other.

Again the Warrior in Jet and Gold tried to cry out, but still Hawkmoon could not hear him. He battled on, desperately trying to reach the Warrior, hacking off a head here, a limb there and slowly coming closer and closer to his mysterious ally.

The Warrior's voice sounded again and this time Hawkmoon heard the words.

"Call for them!" he boomed. "Call for the Legion of the Dawn, Hawkmoon, or we're lost!"

Hawkmoon frowned. "What do you mean?"

"It is your right to command the Legion. Summon them. In the name of the Runestaff, man, *summon them!*"

Hawkmoon parried a thrust and cut down the man who attacked him. The blade's light seemed to be fading, but it could have been that it was now in competition with the scores of torches that blazed in the hall.

"Call for your men, Hawkmoon!" cried the Warrior in Jet and Gold desperately.

Hawkmoon shrugged and, disbelievingly, called out: "I summon the Legion of the Dawn!"

Nothing happened. Hawkmoon had expected nothing. He had no faith in legends, as he had said before.

But then he noticed that the pirates were screaming and that new figures had appeared from nowhere – strange figures who blazed with rosy light, who struck about them ferociously, chopping down the pirates.

Hawkmoon drew a deep breath and wondered at the sight.

The newcomers were dressed in highly ornamental armor that looked somehow of a past age. They were armed with lances decorated with tufts of dyed hair, with huge notched clubs covered with ornate carvings and they howled and shouted and killed with incredible ferocity, driving many pirates from the hall within moments.

Their bodies were brown, their faces covered in paint from which huge black eyes stared, and from their throats came a strange, moaning dirge.

139

The pirates fought back desperately, striking down the shining warriors. But as a man died, his body vanished and a new warrior would appear from nowhere. Hawkmoon tried to see where they came from, but he was never able to do so – he would turn his head and when he looked back a new warrior would be standing there.

Panting, Hawkmoon joined his friends. The naked bodies of Bewchard and D'Averc were cut in a dozen places, but not badly. They stood and watched as the Legion of the Dawn slaughtered the pirates.

"These are the soldiers who serve the sword," said the Warrior in Jet and Gold. "With them, because it then suited the Runestaff's scheme of things, Valjon's ancestor made himself feared throughout Narleen and its surrounds. But now the sword turns against Valjon's people, to take from them what it gave them!"

Hawkmoon felt something touch his ankle, turned and shouted in horror. "The things from the pit! I had forgotten them!" He hacked at the tentacle with his sword and backed away.

Instantly there were a dozen of the shining warriors between him and the monsters. The tufted lances rose and fell, the clubs battered and the monsters tried to retreat. But the Soldiers of the Dawn would not let them retreat. They surrounded them, stabbing and hacking until all that remained was a black mess staining the floor of the hall.

"It is done," Bewchard said incredulously. "We are the victors. The power of Starvel is broken at last." He stooped and picked up a brand. "Come, friend Hawkmoon, let us lead your ghostly warriors forward into the city. Let us kill all we find. Let us burn."

"Aye . . ." Hawkmoon began, but the Warrior in Jet and Gold shook his head.

"No – it is not for killing pirates that the Legion is yours, Hawkmoon. It is yours so that you may do the Runestaff's work."

Hawkmoon hesitated.

The Warrior placed a hand on Bewchard's shoulder. "Now that most of the pirate lords are dead and Valjon destroyed, there will be nothing to stop you and your men returning to Starvel to finish the work we began tonight. But Hawkmoon and his blade are needed for greater things. He must leave soon."

Hawkmoon felt anger come then. "I am grateful to you, Warrior in Jet and Gold, for what you have done to aid me. But I would remind you that I would not be here at all had it not been for your schemings and those of dead Mygan of Llandar. I need to return home – to Castle Brass and my beloved. I am my own man, Warrior – my own man! *I* will decide my own fate."

And then the Warrior in Jet and Gold laughed. "You are still an innocent, Dorian Hawkmoon. You are the Runestaff's man, believe me. You thought you came to this temple merely to help a friend who needed you. But it is the Runestaff's way to work thus! You would not have dared the Pirate Lords had you simply been trying to get the Sword of the Dawn, in whose legend you did not believe, but you did dare them to rescue Bewchard here. The web the Runestaff weaves is a complicated web. Men are never aware of the purposes of their actions where the Runestaff is concerned. Now you must continue on the second part of your mission in Amarehk. You must journey north – you can go round the coast, for Bewchard, I am sure, will lend you a ship – and find Dnark, the City of the Great Good Ones who will need your aid. There you will find proof that the Runestaff exists."

"I am not interested in mysteries, Warrior. I want to know what has become of my wife and friends. Tell me – do we exist in the same era?"

"Aye," said the Warrior. "This time is concurrent with the time you left in Europe. But as you know, Castle Brass exists elsewhere . . ."

"I know that." Hawkmoon frowned thoughtfully. "Well, Warrior, perhaps I will agree to take Bewchard's ship and go on to Dnark. Perhaps . . ."

The Warrior nodded. "Come," he said, "let us leave this unclean place and make our way back to Narleen. There we can discuss with Bewchard the matter of a ship."

Bewchard smiled. "Anything, Hawkmoon, that I have is yours, for you have done much for me and the whole of my city. You saved my life and you were responsible for destroying Narleen's age-old enemies – you may have twenty ships if you wish them."

Hawkmoon was thinking deeply. He had it in mind to deceive the Warrior in Jet and Gold.

Chapter Eleven
THE PARTING

BEWCHARD ESCORTED THEM next afternoon to the quay-side. Everywhere the citizens were celebrating. A force of soldiers had invaded Starvel and routed out every last pirate.

Bewchard put his hand on Hawkmoon's arm. "I wish that you would stay, friend Hawkmoon. We shall be having celebrations for a week yet – and you and your friends should be here. It will be sad for me, celebrating without your company – for you are the true heroes of Narleen, not I."

"We were lucky, Captain Bewchard. It was our good fortune that our fates were linked. You are rid of your enemies – and we have obtained that which we sought." Hawkmoon smiled. "We must leave now."

Bewchard nodded. "If you must, you must." He looked frankly at Hawkmoon and grinned. "I do not suppose that you still believe I am entirely convinced by your story of a 'scholar relative' interested in that sword you now wear?"

Hawkmoon laughed. "No – but on the other hand, captain, I can give you no better story. I do not know why I had to find the sword . . ." He patted the scabbard that now held the Sword of the Dawn. "The Warrior in Jet and Gold here says that it is all part of a larger destiny. Yet I am an unwilling slave to that destiny. All I seek is a little love, a little peace, and to be re-venged upon those who have ravaged my homeland. Yet here I am, on a continent thousands of miles away from where I desire to be, off to seek another legendary object – and reluctantly. Perhaps we shall all understand these matters in time."

Bewchard looked at him seriously. "I think you serve a great purpose, Hawkmoon. I think your destiny is a noble one."

Hawkmoon laughed. "And yet I do not pine for a noble

142

destiny – merely a secure one."

"Perhaps," said Bewchard. "Perhaps. Now, my friend, my best ship is prepared for you and well-provisioned. Narleen's finest sailors have begged to sail with you and now man her. Good luck in your quest, Hawkmoon – and you, too, D'Averc."

D'Averc coughed into his hand. "If Hawkmoon is an unwilling servant of this 'greater destiny,' then what does that make me? A great fool, perhaps? I am unwell, I have a chronically poor constitution, and yet find myself dragged about the world in the service of this mythical Runestaff. Still, it kills time, I suppose."

Hawkmoon smiled, then turned almost anxiously to mount the gangplank of the ship. The Warrior in Jet and Gold moved impatiently.

"Dnark, Hawkmoon," he said. "You must seek the Runestaff itself in Dnark."

"Aye," said Hawkmoon. "I heard you, Warrior."

"The Sword of the Dawn is needed in Dnark," continued the Warrior in Jet and Gold, "and you are needed to wield it."

"Then I shall do as you desire, Warrior," Hawkmoon replied lightly. "Do you sail with us?"

"I have other matters to attend to."

"We shall meet again, doubtless."

"Doubtless."

D'Averc coughed and raised his hand. "Then, farewell, Warrior. Thanks for your aid."

"Thank you for yours," replied the Warrior enigmatically.

Hawkmoon gave the order for the gangplank to be raised and the oars to be unshipped.

Soon the ship was pulling out of the bay and into the open sea. Hawkmoon watched the figures of Bewchard and the Warrior in Jet and Gold become smaller and smaller and smaller and then he turned and smiled at D'Averc.

"Well, D'Averc, do you know where we are going?"

"To Dnark, I take it," D'Averc replied innocently.

"To Europe, D'Averc. I care not for this destiny I'm constantly plagued with. I wish to see my wife again. We are going to sail across the sea, D'Averc – sail for Europe. There we may use our rings to take us back to Castle Brass. I would see Yisselda again."

D'Averc said nothing, merely turned his head to look

143

upward as the white sails billowed and the ship began to gather speed.

"What do you say to that, D'Averc?" Hawkmoon asked with a grin, slapping his friend on the back.

D'Averc shrugged. "I say that it would be a welcome rest to spend some time in Castle Brass again."

"There is something about your tone, friend. Something a trifle sardonic . . ." Hawkmoon frowned. "What is it?"

D'Averc gave him a sidelong glance that matched his tone. "Aye – aye, maybe I am not as sure as you, Hawkmoon, that this ship will find its way to Europe. Perhaps I have a greater respect for the Runestaff."

"You – you believe in legends like that. Why, Amarehk was supposed to be a place of godlike people. It was far from that, eh?"

"I think you insist on the Runestaff's non-existence too much. I think your anxiety to see Yisselda must influence you very strongly."

"Possibly."

"Well, Hawkmoon," said D'Averc, staring out to sea. "Time will tell us how strong the Runestaff is."

Hawkmoon gave him a puzzled look and then shrugged, walking away down the deck.

D'Averc smiled, shaking his head as he watched his friend.

Then he turned his attention to the sails, wondering privately if he would ever see Castle Brass again.